# THE BITTER NIGHT

The Britton boys were already wanted for robbery and murder—$50,000 would be good traveling company to the Mexican border. Sam Kerwin was married to a young and restless wife—$50,000 would go a long way to keep her interested. Harlan Wells had trouble with the bank—$50,000 looked like an easy out. Glen Logan's job was simple—to get the money to the bank. To stay alive was another matter...

# THE BITTER NIGHT

## Wayne D. Overholser, 1906-

**CURLEY LARGE PRINT**
HAMPTON, NEW HAMPSHIRE

*A -1*

**Library of Congress Cataloging-in-Publication Data**

Overholser, Wayne D., 1906–
  The bitter night / Wayne D. Overholser.
  p.   (large print) cm.
  ISBN  0–7927–1787–2
  ISBN  0–7927–1786–4  (pbk.)
  1. Large type books.   I. Title.
[PS3529.V33B58   1933]                                    93–5485
813′.54—dc20                                              CIP

**British Library Cataloguing in Publication Data available**

This Large Print edition is published by Chivers Press, England, and by Curley Large Print, an imprint of Chivers North America, 1993.

Published in the U.S. by arrangement with the Golden West Literary Agency and in the U.K. with Laurence Pollinger, Ltd.

U.K. Hardcover  ISBN  0 7451 2044 X
U.K. Softcover  ISBN  0 7451 2056 3
U.S. Hardcover  ISBN  0 7927 1787 2
U.S. Softcover  ISBN  0 7927 1786 4

*Printed in Great Britain*

# CHAPTER ONE

Glen Logan finished tightening the cinch on his horse and was backing him out of the stall into the runway of the livery stable when Pete Doane, the Gold City marshal, came through the archway from the street. He called, 'Hold on, Glen. I've got to talk to you.'

Glen swore under his breath. He was late getting out of town now. This had been one of those days when everything had gone wrong in his hotel, the last being a fight which had made a shambles out of his barroom. As usual, Pete wasn't on hand when he was needed, so Glen had stopped it himself and thrown the two miners into the street. That had made him half mad, and now to have the garrulous marshal hold him up when he should be riding completed the job.

'I had to throw a couple of drunks out of my place when they got into a scrap,' Glen said. 'That's your job, but you were down the street running off at the mouth. Now just get out of my way because I'm—'

'You're going to see Susan, ain't you?' Doane demanded.

'You know I am,' Glen snapped. 'I go every Saturday afternoon earlier than this.

1

I'd have got away an hour ago if you'd been on Main Street where you belong.'

'All right, all right,' Doane said testily, 'but you're wrong. I wasn't down the street running off at the mouth. I was in the bank. Now shut up and listen.' He cocked his head, his gaze running down Glen's lanky, muscular body, then he said, 'I guess you're man enough to take care of any scraps that start in your place.'

'Damn it, it's your job,' Glen said.

'Sure, but I had another job today. Ed Thorn just shot hisself.'

Doane stopped to let that soak in. The news was important enough to knock the impatience out of Glen. Ed Thorn had been the bank cashier for years. Lately he had been gambling and losing too much in Glen's place as well as the other bars up and down Main Street. More than that, Glen knew that the bank examiner had arrived in town yesterday.

'I thought that would cool you off a mite,' Doane said smugly. 'Now I'll tell you some other things. I got a wire this morning that the Britton boys broke out of the county jail in Cerro along with some small fry. What's more, we've got fifty thousand dollars in cash coming in for the bank on the stage tonight. All right, now you add it up.'

'Maybe you'd better add it up for me,' Glen said. 'I don't like the answer I get when

2

I do the adding.'

'You'll like my answer worse,' Doane said. 'They knew yesterday that something was wrong. With all this talk that's been going around about Thorn's gambling, folks have been getting leery about the bank. A few came in yesterday and took their money out. There was more today. There's more talk going around, too. That's why they sent for so much cash. They finally pinned it on Thorn, all right, and had just sent for me to arrest him when he excused hisself to go to the out-house. He got as far as his coat and shot hisself through the head. Now they ain't sure how much is missing, but it's a hell of a lot.'

Doane pointed his forefinger at Glen like a pistol. 'Here's where you come in. Bronc Kline is driving that stage, and Reno Moore's riding shotgun. They're good men, but they might need help and I figure you're it, seeing as you'll meet the stage at Susan's place. You ride into town with 'em. If that dinero don't get here, we'll have the damnedest run on the bank come Monday morning you ever seen. The bank will go busted and you know what that'd mean to Gold City.'

Glen knew, all right. His money was in the bank along with the cash of almost every businessman in town. Gold City would be ruined. The suffering that would follow was

3

beyond his imagination. He had been in communities where banks had gone broke and he knew what it meant.

The mines would close down, for a time at least. They were owned by local men, small operators who couldn't stand the loss that a bankrupt bank would cause them. With no payroll, there would be starving children in Gold City before the week was out. Bill Buckner who owned the bank would probably make the losses good in time, but he wouldn't be able to immediately.

'All right,' Glen said. 'I'll be on that stage.'

'I figured you would,' Doane said. 'I never knowed you to turn down a dangerous job. Now maybe there ain't no connection between the money and the Britton boys busting out of jail, but on the other hand, there might be. If I had my druthers, I'd just as soon have Butch Cassidy and the Wild Bunch holding up the stage as the Brittons.'

Glen nodded. He had never seen the Britton boys, but he knew them by reputation. The older one named Jake was smart and tough, and the younger one, Bud, was no more than a kid but was as cold-blooded a killer as had ever ridden the owlhoot.

'How'd they get out?' Glen asked.

'This morning they had a gun,' Doane answered. 'When the jailer brought 'em breakfast, they made him unlock the cells

4

and turn everybody loose, then they locked him up. I'm wondering if Ed Thorn might have got it to 'em, figuring he was gonna be found out and if he wasn't arrested right away, maybe he'd get something out of the holdup. We know he left town soon as he got off work yesterday. If they'd told me what was up, I'd have trailed him, but Thorn had worked for Bill Buckner for years, and I guess Bill just didn't think he'd do a thing like that.'

'He could have ridden to Cerro and got back by daylight,' Glen said thoughtfully.

'Only he didn't,' Doane said. 'I seen him playing poker in the Big Horn when I made my rounds last night about ten. Maybe somebody else slipped the Brittons the gun and they don't know nothing about the money.'

'They'll be broke,' Glen said as he stepped into the saddle. 'Chances are they'll hit the stage just on general principles unless they kept going to stay ahead of the sheriff.'

'Naw,' Doane said. 'That fat sheriff in Cerro don't like to ride. According to the story I got over the wire, they stole some horses from the livery stable and hit the breeze out of town, going east. You know that hardpan out there? Well, I guess the sheriff was slow getting out of Cerro and he lost the trail 'bout two miles from town. Now the Britton boys might have kept going east, or they might have circled back once they figured the sheriff was off their tail.'

'I reckon we'll soon know,' Glen said, and rode into the street.

He noticed the storm to the north as he left town. It didn't seem particularly unusual, although the weather had turned inordinately warm the last three days. More than one of the old-timers who hung around the lobby of Glen's hotel had nodded his head sagely and said, 'Just ain't natural to be so danged hot in this country. We're bound to get the damnedest gully washer you ever seen.'

Now the gully washer was on the way, Glen thought as he rode up the twisting switchbacks that rose about Gold City to the summit of Storm Mountain. He stopped on top to blow his horse, his gaze turning again to the north. He had seen high country storms before, but never one that looked like this. In spite of himself, a prickle raced down his spine and spread out into his belly as if it were a live thing eating its way through his bowels.

He shivered, leaning forward in his saddle, one hand on the horn. He guessed the temperature had dropped at least thirty degrees since he'd left Gold City, maybe more. The wind, slashing in from the high peaks at the head of Sundown River, was heavy and damp with the rain that must be coming down in sheets.

He remembered he had been sweating when he'd talked to Pete Doane in the livery stable, his shirt sticking to his skin. He wasn't sweating now, but the front of his shirt was pressed against his chest by the driving wind. It felt as clammy as a shroud, and again he shivered.

He sat staring at the sky, fascinated by it. He wasn't a man to scare easily, but he was scared now, and that was what fascinated him. The thunder he was hearing was no different from other thunder he'd heard a thousand times in the three years he'd owned and operated the hotel in Gold City. Neither was the lightning that raced across the sky, stabbing at the earth as it made its twisting sulfurous pattern, so close it seemed he could almost reach out and touch it.

He wasn't sure what it was that bothered him. Perhaps it was the color of the sky, a weird blue-black curtain that was moving swiftly toward him. It seemed as if the whole north half of the world had been blotted out, as if the earth had risen and the sky descended until they became one and now was moving down upon him, smothering all life before it.

Untying his slicker from behind the saddle, he put it on. He laughed at himself as the thought struck him that maybe Old Scratch was throwing rocks at God and God was tossing thunderbolts back. Since neither was strong enough to win, they'd joined up. That, Glen decided, was bound to be a hell of a strong combination.

He turned his horse and rode down the east slope of Storm Mountain toward Sundown Canyon. He had other things to think about than Old Scratch and God joining forces, other things than the fifty thousand dollars the stage was bringing to Gold City and the Britton boys breaking jail.

Susan Girard, for instance. A more pleasant subject, and a more painful one, too. They had been engaged for a year and there was no reason in the world why they couldn't get married. He loved her with a depth of emotion that was almost terrifying. He didn't doubt that she loved him; he could not doubt it, for doubting would take away his reason for living.

The only excuse she had ever given him for putting off their wedding was that a girl with a father like hers had no right to get married and saddle a husband with him. Well, Matt Girard was the most worthless, lying, sneaking bastard Glen had ever met and that was a fact, but it wasn't the point. Nobody could hold a girl responsible for her father, especially one she had never seen in her life until he'd ridden up less than a year ago and announced who he was.

Susan's place on Black Mesa was a

roadhouse where folks occasionally stayed overnight, but her dining room brought in most of her income. The eastbound stage to Cerro stopped there for dinner, and the westbound stage to Gold City stopped for supper. She made good money, but she worked too hard. She wouldn't quit, so Glen had decided there must be some other reason than her father. Since he didn't have any idea what it was, he worried about it.

The rain hit him before he was halfway down the long grade to the bridge that crossed Sundown River. He pulled his hatbrim lower over his eyes and hunched his shoulders forward. The clouds had raced across the sky and covered the sun so that now an eerie half-light shrouded the cedar-covered mountain, giving Glen the feeling that night was settling down before five o'clock in the afternoon. The rain swept past him in a solid sheet, eased off, and came again as if someone was filling a giant tub and dumping it and repeating the process over and over.

The Sundown would be a boiling torrent, he thought. Downstream on the plains it would be over its banks, cutting new channels and washing out the farms and ditches that were close to it, but Susan's place set on Black Mesa east of the river was too high to be hurt.

The rain didn't stop when he reached the

bottom of the grade. If anything, it came down harder than ever. He heard a great rumble upstream, but he could not identify the sound. At the moment he didn't give a second thought to it, for his horse was nervous and he had trouble getting the animal on the bridge.

The water was high and roily as he knew it would be, but the bridge seemed safe enough. When he was halfway across, the rumble became deafening. He glanced upstream. He saw a wall of water ten feet high sweep around a bend in the river, tossing giant pine trees about as if they were matches.

For one terrifying moment Glen couldn't breathe, so great was the pressure against his chest. He had the feeling that time was suspended, that he was caught in the path of the flood without power to move. His heart was somewhere below his stomach, then the paralysis passed, and he slashed his horse with his spurs.

The animal lunged forward, hoofs striking hard against the wet planks, skidding and sliding, and again Glen had the feel he was held here, moving in slow, deliberate motion when only speed could save his and the horse's life. All the time that wall of water with its load of heaving logs was pouring down upon the bridge like a battering-ram.

He was ten feet from the east side and

10

safety, then five. He heard the first log slam into the bridge: he heard the creaking and groaning of timbers and felt the shivering of the bridge as it began to give under the pressure of the flood. The horse's hoofs hit the dirt of the road, another great lunge carried him on up the steep slope just as the center of the bridge gave way and swung downstream.

Still the horse fought for footing in the mud. Glen had thought they were safely across, but now it seemed that nothing could keep his mount from sliding back down the slope into the muddy, foaming water. Again he dug his spurs into the flanks of the frightened animal. Another lunge, and with his great muscles straining, the grunting, floundering horse reached the level above the river and stood there trembling.

Glen glanced back, his body weak with relief. Only heaving logs and water heavy with silt where the bridge had been. He sat his saddle for a long moment, having trouble with his breathing, then he rode on up the grade to the top of Black Mesa.

Glen told himself bitterly that it didn't make much difference where the Britton boys were or what they did. Nature had decreed that the stage wouldn't be going through tonight. Or tomorrow. Perhaps not for another week. It would take at least that long to repair the bridge.

By now the news that Ed Thorn had shot himself would be all over Gold City. Gossip would make the most of it and panic would sweep the mining camp. Before dawn Monday the depositors would be pounding on the bank's doors demanding their money. If the fifty thousand dollars the stage was carrying wasn't in the bank safe by nine o'clock Monday morning, the bank would go under, and then there'd be hell to pay.

## CHAPTER TWO

From her kitchen window Susan Girard could see the high peaks in which Sundown River had its source. All afternoon she had watched the clouds gather up there and then sweep south toward Storm Mountain and spread toward the plains until the sky was covered. She saw the lightning leap downward, lashing one granite point after another; she heard the thunder, but the storm seemed distant and unimportant to her, so she gave little thought to it.

Actually one mountain storm was just about the same as another. They nearly always started this way; they would work downslope until they struck her place with high country ferocity and then as often as not they would blow themselves out in a matter of minutes, the sun would appear again, and she would be thankful for the shower that had brought its damp coolness to the mesa.

So today she saw nothing unusual about this storm except that the sky had turned abnormally black, a strange, almost unearthly darkness that frightened her a little. Then she decided it was a cloudburst above timberline that would soon move southward and be out of sight.

She began peeling potatoes for supper. The stage was due at six and it was getting on toward five. She never knew how many to expect, but at least there would be the driver, Bronc Kline, and Reno Moore, the shotgun guard. The Tuckers, of course, Molly who worked in the house with her, and Joe who did the chores and took care of the horses for the stage company. She could count on three passengers, if an average meant anything. And, today being Saturday, she would set a plate for Glen Logan.

Glen would be here about five, at least by six. He rode down from Gold City to see her every Saturday regardless of the weather or other commitments. She didn't know what she would do if he failed to come some Saturday. He was steadfast, he was faithful, he was her strength. More than that, she loved him.

He was always in her mind a great deal these moments on Saturday afternoon just before he came, moments that were bittersweet because she felt so strongly the need to see him, to be kissed by him, to be held in his strong arms, yet the pleasure that came from being with him was diluted by the knowledge she could not go on dangling him the way she had been doing or she would lose him. She would hear the inevitable question, 'When are we getting married, Sue?' And she would give her equally inevitable answer, 'I don't know, Glen, but it won't be long.'

She finished the potatoes and put them on the stove, then the rain struck, the gusty wind shaking the house and rattling the windows. Molly Tucker was sitting on the other side of the kitchen table stringing beans that had been picked from the garden that morning.

'Goodness, listen to it.' Molly jumped up and set the pan of beans on the table. 'I'll run upstairs and put the windows down. This is a corker.'

Susan raced from one window to another in the downstairs rooms, then mopped the floor under the west windows. A moment later Molly came back down the stairs for the mop, moving as fast as her great bulk permitted.

'I seen that storm coming,' she said, angry at herself, 'but I never dreamt it would be this bad or would get here so quick. I guess

14

the good Lord pulled the cork out of the sky and turned on the faucet.'

By the time she returned the second time, Susan had finished stringing the beans and had them in a pan on the stove. She said, 'We should have brought in more wood. If this keeps up, we'll have to get some and we'll be soaked before we're halfway to the woodshed.'

'I'd go after Joe, but it's ten times as far to the barn.' Molly stared out of the rain-streaked window, her moonlike face turning sour. 'Sometimes I wonder why I keep living with that no-good Joe and why you keep on paying him. I get so mad at him that I think I could choke him. He never brings in enough wood to get us through supper.' Then her face brightened. 'Susie, maybe Glen will get here in time to bring the wood in for us.'

'I won't ask him,' Susan said.

'He wouldn't mind.' Molly stopped, her big head cocked to one side. 'What was that?'

Susan had heard the noise, but she hadn't identified it, either. It sounded as if the wind had picked up a heavy object and slammed it down on the back porch. For a moment Susan hesitated, then she walked to the door. To open it was asking for a soaking, the way the wind was sweeping the rain across the porch.

15

'Don't go out there, honey,' Molly cried. 'You'll get wet the minute you poke your nose...'

'I've been wet before,' Susan said, and opening the door stepped through it.

The wind struck her in a great gust, soaking her with a solid sheet of water, much of it from the gutter at the far corner of the porch roof. For a moment she stood staring at the man who lay face down on the porch, the rain beating at her. Her father! Of all times, why did he have to come today? She ran to him and knelt beside him. His horse stood head down at the corner of the house, his rump to the wind.

She tried to turn him over but he was too heavy. He was like a two-hundred-pound sack of grain. She screamed, 'Molly! Come and help me, Molly.'

Molly poked her head through the door. 'I'm not going to get wet just because...' Then she recognized the motionless man. 'What's Matt doing here?'

'I don't know, but he's unconscious,' Susan cried. 'Come on. Help me.'

Grumbling that she guessed she'd been wet before too, she took hold of one of Matt Girard's shoulders and Susan the other. Together they dragged his big body into the kitchen and on into Susan's bedroom. Molly straightened up and putting a hand to her back, stared disgustedly at the motionless

16

man.

'Talk about bad pennies coming back,' she said. 'Why can't he fall off a cliff or get drowned or something like he deserves?'

Susan didn't answer, but the same question had often occurred to her. She was ashamed of herself, yet the truth was she never wanted to see her father again. But here he was and she would probably have to give him more money to leave, money which she knew would never be returned.

'We've got to get him on the bed,' Susan said. 'Do you suppose we can lift his shoulders to the bed and then...'

'Nope,' Molly said in her positive tone. 'He's a no-good spalpeen and you know it, and I ain't gonna break my back on him. Let him lie there. I'm going to change my clothes. We've got to get them biscuits in the oven. 'Bout time we basted that roast, too.'

She swung around and walked to the door, then stopped. 'Susan, the last time Matt was here, Joe told him he'd twist his neck just like a rooster for Sunday dinner if he ever showed up again. He might do it, too. He's told Matt often enough to stay away and quit sponging off of you.'

'I can't throw him out into the rain,' Susan protested. 'He's sick or something.'

'Or drunk,' Molly snorted.

'Don't tell Joe he's here,' Susan said.

'He'll find out for himself soon enough,'

17

Molly said somberly, and left the room.

Susan changed into dry clothes. She knelt on the floor beside Matt and shook him. She found a towel and wiped his face, then she tried to pull his boots off but she couldn't. For several minutes she knelt beside him, staring at his rough-featured face. Strange, she thought, that he would come back to haunt her after all these years.

She had never been told the whole story by her mother, but from the fragments she had pieced together, she knew most of what had happened. Apparently Matt Girard had deserted Susan's mother shortly after they were married. Susan wasn't sure whether he knew his wife was pregnant or not. In any case, he never came back. Susan's mother married a man named Paul Kelsey who was steady and a hard worker, and to all intents and purposes was Susan's father.

The Kelseys came here nine years ago and operated the roadhouse, raised horses, and ran a few cows. They hired Joe and Molly Tucker, they were prosperous, saving a thousand dollars or more a year and burying it in a bucket in the yard. In other ways Paul Kelsey had been a normal, rational man, but in his distrust of banks he was, as Susan's mother said frankly, simply 'tetched.'

The fact that he had more than five thousand dollars hidden in his yard must have leaked out, although Susan never knew

18

how. Three years ago two men rode in one day when the Tuckers were gone, locked Susan up in the storeroom, and tortured her mother until she told them where the money was hidden.

The men shot and killed Paul Kelsey and Susan's mother, took the money and rode away. By the time the Tuckers returned and released Susan and Joe got word to the sheriff at Cerro, the outlaws were out of the country.

Susan often wondered why she hadn't been killed, too. She had seen the men and thought she would recognize them if she ever met them again. The older one had been nineteen or twenty, very tall and slender, the second had been no more than a kid, fifteen or sixteen, as smooth-faced as a girl and quite small. Susan hadn't heard the young one say a word and had often wondered whether he was a boy or a girl dressed as a boy.

Susan stayed on, running the place much as Kelsey and her mother had done except that she had sold off the cattle and raised fewer horses than Paul Kelsey had. Joe and Molly Tucker had stayed with her. She could not ask for better help than Molly, and although Joe was proddy and sullen with other people, he had been good to her.

If Matt Girard had not showed up less than a year ago, she would have married

Glen before this. Perhaps she could have persuaded him to sell his hotel and bar in Gold City and move in with her here. He was a good hand with cattle, and it had been her dream to go back into the business when she had the money to buy good stock and had good help.

But Matt had come, pretending he was glad he had found his daughter when actually the only reason he had for being glad was that she was an easy mark and he could sponge off her just as Molly had said. Now, staring at his whiskery face, Susan told herself this was the last time she would give him anything.

Her sense of obligation to a long-lost father was just as misguided as Glen had said. She owed Matt nothing. He had promised to quit drinking and get a job, but it always turned out the same way. He'd go away with fifty or sixty dollars that Susan had given him, maybe trade an ancient, worthless saddle horse for one of Susan's, which made Joe Tucker furious, and within a month or six weeks he'd be back and they would go through the same procedure again.

To this day Susan did not know how Matt had found her. He was always evasive when she asked him. He claimed he knew her mother was living with a man named Paul Kelsey and he'd heard Kelsey had been murdered. Perhaps the story was true, perhaps not. It didn't seem important. What was important was that she could not marry Glen as long as Matt was a burden to her. He had no conscience, she told herself; he would find some way to use her as a lever to sponge off Glen, maybe blackmail him. Matt would not be above doing such a thing if he stumbled upon something he could use against Glen.

She would marry him, she thought. Tomorrow if he wanted to. They'd both sell out and leave the country. Matt would never find them. That was the way it would have to be if they were to have any chance for a happy marriage.

She shook Matt again, but apparently he was still unconscious. A pool of water had formed on the floor all around him. Maybe he would get pneumonia and die. For the first time since Matt had come into her life she was not ashamed of the thought.

Molly opened the door. 'Better give me a hand with supper,' she said. 'Besides, I just seen Glen ride to the barn.'

'Coming,' Susan said, and stood up.

For a moment she looked down at Matt, feeling only contempt for him and wondering why she had ever felt she owed him anything because he was her father. Turning, she left the room, closing the door behind her.

# CHAPTER THREE

The rain had slacked off by the time Glen reached Black Mesa. He rode into the barn, dismounted and taking off his slicker, hung it on a nail. He glanced at his watch. Nearly six. The Gold City stage would be in any time.

From where Glen stood just inside the big double doors, he saw the top of Joe Tucker's head over the wall of a stall about halfway along the runway. He was harnessing the horses that were supposed to take the stage across Sundown River and on over Storm Mountain to Gold City.

He should tell Tucker the bridge was out, Glen thought. Tucker might as well start taking the harness off the horses, but perversely Glen stood motionless. Tucker knew he was there, for he had turned his head, glanced at him, and then had given him his back. This was exactly like Tucker, Glen thought. The man hated him. In fact, he seemed to hate everyone except himself, his wife, and Susan.

Leading his horse into the nearest stall, Glen unsaddled him, rubbed him down, and fed him. According to Glen's book, Joe Tucker was strictly no good, and Susan's reason for keeping him eluded Glen, unless it was that she had to give Tucker work in order to keep his wife Molly. In a way it made sense, for Molly was worth far more than Susan could pay her, but Molly's reason for continuing to live with Tucker was completely beyond Glen. It seemed impossible for any woman, even one with a heart as big as Molly's, to love a man like Joe Tucker.

When Glen stepped out of the stall into the runway, Tucker was waiting for him. He said, 'Logan, you've got a damned thick head. I told you last week to stay away from Susan. She's too good for the likes of you.'

Glen rammed his hands into his pockets and looked Tucker over from his round, bald head down the thick wedge of his body to his inordinately small feet incased in expensive, spike-heeled boots. He was an ugly man with a fat nose and a pendulous-lipped mouth, having nothing to be vain about except his small feet.

Glen raised his gaze to Tucker's tiny, red eyes. He said, 'Joe, you're right about Susan being too good for the likes of me, but I'll keep on seeing her until she tells me to stop. I sure as hell won't stop because an ugly bastard like you tells me to.'

Tucker took a step forward, his face turning scarlet. Then he stopped, thick shoulders hunched forward, his big hands fisting and opening and fisting again at his sides. He had been aching for a fight with Glen for weeks. The only reason Glen hadn't obliged him was the knowledge that it would hurt Susan. For some reason Tucker gave Susan a strange, unquestioning loyalty. Perhaps that was part of the reason she kept him.

Now Tucker fought his temper, finally saying, 'She ain't got the gall to tell you. She's too big-hearted to hurt anybody, so I'll do the telling. She ain't for you. Now I'm giving you three minutes to get that saddle back on your horse and ride out.'

'What difference does it make to you whether I see Susan or not?' Glen asked. 'I aim to marry her, in case you're questioning my intentions.'

'Sure you'd like to marry her, but I ain't gonna stand for it,' Tucker said. 'Molly'n me don't have no children. Susan's the next thing to it and I don't figure on letting her go on working herself to death feeding a stage full of pilgrims twice a day. I'm gonna have a lot of dinero one of these times, and when I do, I'm taking her a long ways from here.'

'I'll do the taking,' Glen said. 'Not you.'

He wheeled and started toward the door. Tucker grabbed him by a shoulder and whirled him around, a big fist raised. Glen yanked free of Tucker's grip just as the big man threw the punch. It missed by a quarter of an inch as Glen jerked his head to one side.

Tucker, pulled off balance by the blow, was wide open. Moving in fast, Glen caught him on the nose with a powerful right. Blood spurted like juice from an overripe plum. Tucker grunted with pain and retreated a step, throwing out his left in a futile defensive motion.

Glen followed his advantage, slamming a right to the man's belly that drove breath out of him, then a left to the mouth that cut a lip and brought another stream of blood flowing down his chin. Tucker staggered, recovered his balance, and blocked Glen's next blow with his forearms. He went in then, connecting with two good punches to Glen's ribs that jolted and hurt. Then he threw out both hands, trying to grab Glen around the waist and drag him down into the straw and manure of the barn floor.

Just as Tucker's arms were closing around Glen's middle, Glen smashed him in the face with a swinging fist that hammered his head back as if he had been struck by a maul. His arms swung apart and he went down, his hands brushing both sides of Glen's pants. As he fell, Glen hit him below the back of the head with a down-driving fist that would have snapped the neck of a less powerful man. He lay motionless at Glen's feet, his face in the litter.

Stooping, Glen rolled him over on his

back. He said, 'Joe, you listen to me and listen good. You're taking orders from Susan, not giving them. Now I'll just tell you one more thing and don't you forget it. You try this again and I'll get rough.'

Tucker lifted himself to one elbow and spit out a mouthful of blood. He wiped his face with a sleeve, drawing a red mask across it. He said thickly, 'Next time, by God, I'll kill you.'

'If you want to live, don't try it,' Glen said, and taking his slicker off the nail, started toward the house.

The rain had almost stopped, but now it came again, rolling across the mesa in a downbeating torrent that spread a silver curtain between the rim and Sundown Canyon, completely hiding Storm Mountain on the west side of the river. Glen pulled on his slicker and ran across the yard to the house, slipping and sliding in the mud. He cleaned his boots on the metal scraper set upright at the edge of the door, and went in.

Susan must have seen him coming, for she was waiting in the hall for him. She threw her arms around him and hugged him hard, ignoring the wet slicker that soaked the front of her dress. 'Glen, Glen,' she said. 'I thought you'd never get here.' She lifted her mouth for his kiss, and then tipped her head back to look at him. Smiling, she whispered, 'I never thought you'd look as good to me as you do this minute.'

He touched her gently on the side of the face. 'Honey, I always hoped that someday you'd meet me like this, but I didn't expect it tonight.'

She was still smiling. 'Ask me again, Glen. I've put you off so many times.'

'I guess it is time for the weekly question,' he agreed. 'When are we getting married?'

'Next month,' she said. 'Next week. Tomorrow. Any day you name.'

He took his hat off and sailed it into the corner where it hooked onto one of the limbs of the hall tree, whirled around, and settled there. 'I'm dreaming,' he said. 'I don't believe you said what I heard.'

'I said it,' she told him. 'All of a sudden I realize that the things which have kept us apart aren't very important. And I've always prided myself on being able to take care of myself. Now I know I've been fooling myself. I need you.'

'We can't get married tomorrow because we can't get to Gold City unless we take horses and swim the river. The bridge went out just after I crossed it.'

'Oh.' She was shocked, then shook her head as she realized what this meant. 'If there's more than ten people on that stage, some of them will have to sleep in the barn.' Then she smiled again. 'It doesn't matter. We'll make out. Right now I need your help.

Pa's here.'

Glen groaned. 'Again?'

She told him what had happened. 'You'll have to lift him to the bed, then get rid of his horse. That's what worries me. You know how Joe hates him. He said he'd kill Pa if he ever came back. I think he will, so we've got to keep him from knowing about Pa being here.'

'It's time you got rid of Tucker,' Glen said. 'Last week he told me to stay away from you, so when I rode in just now, he jumped me and I had to whip him.'

He sensed the misery that was in her when she looked at him, then she turned her head. 'I'll fire him,' she said. 'I should have done it a long time ago. I would have if it hadn't been for Molly. I can't get along without her.' She turned her head to look at him, taking hold of his hands. 'But I've got to keep Joe until I get another man. Right now Pa's here and I'm afraid of what will happen if Joe finds out.'

'I'll see Matt,' Glen said, 'and then we'll decide what to do with the horse. We'll have to take one job at a time.'

She glanced through the door into the parlor at the pendulum clock on the wall. 'It's almost six. Bronc isn't usually late.'

'The rain's held him up tonight,' Glen said. 'Which room is your pa in?'

'Mine.'

He strode past her along the hall and into the kitchen. Glancing into the dining room, he saw that the long table was set. When he reached the range, he paused to watch Molly lift the roast out of the oven.

'Howdy, Molly,' he said. 'Smells good in here.'

'Ought to,' she said. 'Susie cooked it. Now where do you suppose that ornry Bronc Kline is? He oughtta be here before now.'

'Likely stuck in the mud. We had a rain in case you didn't notice.'

'No, I didn't notice,' Molly snapped. 'I'm deaf, dumb, and blind. Well, he'd better get out of the mud 'cause supper's ready and my biscuits ain't good if they set and dry out.'

Susan said, 'The bridge is out, Molly. We'll have to put everybody up for the night.'

Molly took a moment to digest that piece of information, then lifted a corner of her apron and wiped her face. 'Now why does everything happen to us?' she groaned. 'Well, I ain't giving my bed up to no pilgrim, and you ain't giving yours up to your sponge of a pa. Throw him out into the rain, Glen.'

'No, Glen,' Susan said. 'He can stay until morning.'

'Honey,' Molly said angrily, 'you just can't go on letting that lazy scamp you've got for a pa go on...'

Glen went on into the bedroom, shutting

the door and cutting off the rest of what Molly said, but judging by the way she started, he was in complete agreement.

## CHAPTER FOUR

When Glen entered Susan's room, he found Matt Girard stretched out on her bed. His eyes were closed, but when he heard the door, he opened them and looked at Glen. He blinked, then shut them quickly as if hoping he could fool Glen into thinking he was still unconscious.

Glen's lips curled in contempt. According to Matt, his big body was always filled with the miseries. Perhaps it was, for he drank too much, a failing that was indicated by his red nose and the network of purple veins that covered his face.

He had a talent for making big plans which were totally impractical; he habitually made promises he could not keep and probably never intended to. Glen could overlook these faults, but he could not overlook the way Matt had taken advantage of Susan from the first time he'd come here and announced he was her father.

'Get up,' Glen said harshly. 'Get up and get on your horse and get to hell out of here.'

'I can't,' Matt whined. 'I'm sick. I don't

know what's wrong with me. I'd been riding all day and that storm caught me. All I remember is getting to Susie's porch and falling down. When I woke up, I was here.'

'You're lying again,' Glen said. 'Susan and Molly dragged you in from the porch but they weren't strong enough to hoist you into bed.'

'I must have got up here myself,' Matt said. 'I just disremember.'

'I don't think you're sick,' Glen said. 'I don't think you fainted. You knew Susan would be sorry for you if she thought you were sick, so you're play-acting again to get her sympathy. You figured you'd wind up getting more money and maybe a fresh horse the way you always have.'

'That ain't so,' Matt protested in an aggrieved tone. 'I just wanted to get a couple of good meals under my belt and some rest. In the morning I'll ride to Gold City. I promise I won't bother Susie no more.'

'You won't be going to Gold City,' Glen told him. 'The bridge washed out.'

'The hell!' Matt sat up on one elbow, apparently jolted by what Glen had told him. 'Then I've got to stay here. I can't go back to Cerro.'

'You're not staying here,' Glen said angrily. 'What did Joe Tucker tell you he'd do if you showed up here again?'

'He said he'd kill me, but I reckon he was

31

joshing.'

'I don't think so. Neither does Susan. How do you think it would make her feel to have you shot right here in her house?'

'It'd make her feel bad, I reckon,' Matt admitted. 'I'd feel bad, too.' He swallowed, and added plaintively, 'But I can't go now.'

'All right, you can stay here tonight, but you're pulling out before sunup in the morning, and you're not leaving this room tonight. Savvy?'

'Sure. I don't want to leave this room. I don't want no trouble with nobody, and I sure don't want to worry Susie. She's a good girl.'

'Oh hell,' Glen said in disgust. 'You don't care how much you worry Susan as long as you can get something out of her. You're a no-good, lazy moocher, Matt. Susan never did anything to deserve you for a father. Why don't you go away and leave her alone?'

'I will,' Matt promised. 'I'll never see her again.' He sighed. 'But it don't seem quite fair, Susie being my only kin and me being all she's got.'

Glen wheeled and walked to the door. No use to talk to Matt. He'd keep coming back as long as Susan was here. She was too good a meal ticket for him to let go.

'I wouldn't be here this time if I'd had anywhere else to go,' Matt went on. 'I was broke when we busted out of jail, Glen. I just didn't have nowhere else to go.'

Glen walked back to the bed. 'You were in jail in Cerro?'

'That's right. I'd been there a couple of days for getting drunk. Five of us got out. That was all who was in the jail. The Britton boys was the ones the sheriff wanted. They headed east. The rest of us scattered. I guess we wasn't worth chasing.'

'How did you get out of jail?'

'Easy. Plumb easy. Jake Britton had a gun. I dunno how he got it, but come morning he had it. When the jailer showed up, Jake shoved the gun into his belly and he opened the cell door.' Matt laughed. 'That Jake has a funny bone. Said he figured the jailer wanted to be alone, so he turned all of us loose and locked the jailer up. Bud now, he don't have a funny bone in him. Mean. Plain mean.'

'Where'd you get your horse?'

'Bought him,' Matt said. 'That's why I'm broke.'

He was lying, but Glen had a feeling that the rest he had said was true. Maybe he'd heard about the fifty thousand dollars that would be on the stage, but maybe he didn't know, so Glen decided not to mention it. Matt had been in jail for various misdemeanors, but as far as Glen knew, he had never committed a felony in his life. Still, the knowledge that he was in the same house with that much money might give courage even to Matt Girard.

'The Brittons say where they were headed?'

'No, but I figure they're still running. They ain't got nothing to gain by hanging around here. They was being held for trial on account of murdering that stage driver, you know. They held up a stage on the other side of Cerro last month. I heard that if the Cerro jury let 'em go, there were five other states that wanted 'em for murder.'

Glen turned toward the door again. 'Stay in this room. Don't leave it for anything.'

'I won't,' Matt promised. 'I sure don't want no trouble with Joe Tucker.'

Glen left the room, closing the door behind him. Susan and Molly were working at the stove. Glen said, 'I told him he had to pull out before sunup. No use trying to hide his horse, Sue. Joe's bound to find him if we try, so I'll take him to the barn and say he drifted in.'

'All right,' Susan said, 'if you think that's the thing to do.'

She glanced at him and tried to smile, but her pale face seemed frozen. She raised a hand to her forehead and brushed back an unruly lock of blonde hair, then turned her attention to the pan of gravy she was stirring.

Glen crossed to the stove. 'Molly, why did Joe threaten to kill Matt if he showed up again?'

Molly glanced quickly at Susan, then turned her back to Glen. Stooping, she took a pan of biscuits out of the oven and set it on the back of the range. Then she turned to face Glen.

'I guess you won't believe me 'cause you think Joe's no account,' Molly said. 'Maybe you're right, judging by some of the things he does, but he's got one decent streak in him. He loves Susan same as I do. We've tried to look out for her ever since her ma and Paul Kelsey got killed. Joe's like the rest of us, mighty tired of seeing Matt bleed Susie white, so he figured maybe he could scare Matt from coming back.'

'He didn't,' Glen said.

'No, and it'll make him mad when he finds out,' Molly said. 'Mad and kind o' crazy, I guess. Crazy enough to do what he said he would.'

'No matter how it hurts Sue?'

'That's right,' Molly said. 'I've seen him when he gets mad that way. Just quits thinking.'

'I've got to fire him,' Susan said. 'I know he likes me, but I've still got to fire him. He had a fight with Glen tonight because he'd told Glen to stay away. He can't make all my decisions for me, Molly.'

'I know,' Molly said bitterly. 'I've seen this coming and I knew that sooner or later that's what you'd have to do. Well, you'd best take

35

that horse to the barn, Glen.'

'I guess I had,' Glen said.

He got his hat from the hall rack, and came back through the kitchen. Matt's horse still stood behind the house, his rump to the driving wind. Glen mounted and rode to the barn.

Tucker was standing in the doorway when Glen stepped down and handed him the reins. 'This horse drifted in. Must have throwed his rider during the storm. Ever seen him before?'

Tucker glanced at the bay gelding and shook his head, then shot a glance at Glen, an expression of sheer animal hatred in his eyes. A clot of blood hung from his nose; his mouth was bruised and swollen where Glen's fist had smashed his lip. He didn't say anything, but he took the reins and led the horse to an empty stall.

Glen thought, *He'll shoot me in the back if he gets a chance.* The notion that he would do anything without a compelling selfish motive seemed ridiculous, and yet he had worked here for several years, first for Kelsey and then for Susan, dirty stable work that had no future and for wages that were lower than he could have made in Gold City. There was no way to judge a man like that, Glen told himself. Molly knew him better than anyone else. She might be right about him, but Glen didn't believe it.

Turning, Glen saw the stage wheel in off the county road. He called, 'Tucker, the stage is coming.'

Tucker stepped out of the stall where he had taken Matt's horse and came along the runway, stubby legs moving in short, quick strides, his long arms swinging at his sides. He looked like a great ape, Glen thought, and would have seemed more at home in the jungles of Africa than here.

'You don't need to change horses,' Glen said. 'The bridge went out.'

Tucker pretended he hadn't heard. He took his slicker off a nail in the wall, put it on, and strode toward the stage that had stopped in front of the house. The driver, Bronc Kline, swung down, calling, 'Half hour for supper stop.'

Glen left the barn, reaching the stage as the last passenger stepped out and hurried toward the house. He was Sam Kerwin, a rancher from above Gold City near the head of the Sundown. Tucker was unhitching the horses. The guard, Reno Moore, was on the ground, his Winchester in his hands. Glen spoke to him and went on to where Bronc Kline stood.

'Howdy, Glen,' Kline said. 'Never miss a Saturday night, do you?'

'Not if I can help it,' Glen answered. 'Bronc, you'll be bedding down here tonight. The bridge went out this afternoon.'

Kline stared at him in the thin light, rain dripping off his nose and the point of his chin. 'The hell,' he said.

Kline was a tall man with strong regular features, his face burned dark by years of exposure to wind and sun. A good jehu, Glen knew, the best on the Cerro-Gold City run, and Reno Moore was the best guard. Carrying big sums of money between the two towns was nothing new to either. Their courage had been tested many times, and now, Glen thought, it would be tested again.

Kline took another moment to digest what Glen had said, then he demanded, 'You sure?'

'I ought to be,' Glen said. 'I damned near got drowned when it went. You won't be taking this coach across tonight or tomorrow.'

Kline cursed, then motioned for Moore to come up. 'We seen that storm boiling up over the mountains when we left Cerro. Must have been a belly snapper.'

'It was,' Glen said, 'and I was right in the big middle of it.' Moore was beside them then. Glen glanced at Tucker, and seeing that he was far enough away so he wouldn't hear, he said in a low tone, 'Pete Doane told me what you're carrying and wanted me to give you a hand. He said the Brittons busted out of jail this morning.'

Kline's grin tightened. 'Glad to have you

aboard, son. I sure wasn't counting on Tucker for any help. Well, that dinero's got to be in Gold City Monday morning before nine o'clock, bridge or no bridge.'

'It will be,' Moore said. 'We can get horses across the river tomorrow.'

'Maybe,' Glen said, 'if it quits raining, and if we're still around and we've still got the money.'

'We'll have it,' Moore said.

Reno Moore was a small, knot-tough man, red-haired and freckle-faced. If it came to a showdown, Glen couldn't have picked two better men.

'Let's lug it inside,' Kline said. 'Might as well tell the passengers the bad news. They ain't gonna like it much.'

Moore pulled the box out from under the seat and Kline took one end, Moore the other. Fifty thousand dollars! A fortune by any standard, Glen thought as he followed them inside, enough of a fortune to make an outlaw out of almost any honest man.


## CHAPTER FIVE

From the top of a small ridge east of Susan Girard's place Jake and Bud Britton had watched the Cerro-Gold City road and Susan's house and barn for a good part of the afternoon. The wait had been a long one, the cold rain and wind adding to their discomfort. The veil of twilight that the storm had laid upon the land was even worse. Bud was superstitious, and this seemed to him a bad omen.

By the time the stage appeared, the nerves of both men had been drawn so tight that they'd begun to snap at each other. Jake was the first to see the coach when it broke into the open below them. He said, 'There it is.'

'It's time,' Bud said.

They grinned at each other, the tension gone. Funny thing, Jake thought. He was the older, twenty-four, and Bud was only nineteen, but they'd been riding the dark trails for the last seven years. The pattern never varied. There was a period of uncertainty before each job, of waiting until the time was exactly right, and nervousness was always a part of the waiting.

Probably the waiting was a good thing, Jake told himself. It kept them alert; it made them careful. He had seen too often what happened when it worked the other way. Outlaws who were too successful often became overconfident and underestimated their opposition. One mistake was all a man was allowed in this business. He had dinned that into Bud as long as they had been operating together, yet he wasn't sure he had ever got it across.

40

'Let's ride,' Bud said.

'Not yet,' Jake told him.

Jake considered his brother as he stroked his black spade beard. It made him look years older than he was, giving him a patriarchal appearance that pleased his vanity. It was one of his biggest assets, making him look like a pious elder in the church rather than a successful outlaw.

Jake was well aware that he was about as different from Bud in both appearance and character as two brothers could be. In one way that was good, but in another and more important way it was bad, for there were times when controlling Bud was like trying to rope the wind.

Bud had killed his first man when he was twelve. Jake had no idea how many his brother had killed since then, but it was too many, far too many. He studied Bud who was unaware of his scrutiny, for he was watching the stage passengers get out of the coach and run through the rain to the house.

Bud was tall and very slender with extraordinarily long fingers. He had the delicate features of a girl, and before he had grown tall a couple of years ago, he had often put on a dress and passed for a girl. It had been an extremely successful disguise, with Jake posing as the girl's father. Bud was fast on the draw, and an accurate shot. Jake was neither. Bud had a mania for killing. Jake hated to kill unless it was a case of necessity.

Bud had another side that didn't make any sense to Jake. At times he was almost a coward, particularly when they ran into one of his superstitions. He would ride a mile out of his way if it meant avoiding the path of a black cat. He wouldn't do anything on the thirteenth of the month. If it happened to be Friday as well as the thirteenth, he'd hide all day.

Anything that Bud interpreted as a bad omen would make him turn around and give up whatever project they had started out to do. For the last two hours Jake had been afraid that was what Bud would do today because of the thin light. Jake told himself angrily that he'd pistol-whip the kid if he did. You couldn't pass up fifty thousand dollars no matter what the omens were, not when it was right here in your lap waiting to be taken.

This would be their last job. They had agreed to that. Their stay in the Cerro jail had convinced them their luck had run out. If they hadn't broken out of jail, they would certainly have stretched rope.

Bud turned his head to find Jake staring at him. 'What's the matter?' he demanded. 'What are you looking at me like that for?'

Jake grinned. 'I wasn't. I mean, I wasn't seeing you. I was thinking about what we can do with that dinero the stage is carrying, and how long it will take us to get to Mexico. Well, guess it's time we headed for the bridge.'

'More'n time,' Bud grunted.

They mounted and angled down the slope to the county road. The footing was treacherous, their horses sliding in the mud. No night for a fast ride, Jake thought, but a fast ride wouldn't be necessary. They'd stop the stage beyond the bridge just as the coach started up the steep pitch on the west side.

They'd take the money and send the stage on to Gold City, then they'd head downstream for a few miles before they cut directly south. The rain would make tracking impossible. The chances were they'd be in New Mexico before the sheriff got on their trail if he ever did.

Suddenly Jake laughed. Bud asked, 'What's funny?'

'I was just thinking 'bout that fat sheriff in Cerro, coming into our cells this morning to tell us how high he was gonna hang us. I'll bet he's still trying to pick up our tracks east of town.'

But Bud didn't see anything funny. He glanced at the dark sky and shivered. Jake knew what he was thinking, and he said savagely, 'By God, Bud, if you walk out on me now, I'll part your hair with the barrel of my gun.'

'All right, all right,' Bud said. 'What about

'horn and Joe Tucker? They're supposed to get a third of what we take.'

Jake snickered. 'They're supposed to, all right. Well, they can have it if they can catch us, but I doubt that they can.'

'If Thorn hadn't told Tucker about the money,' Bud said, 'and if Tucker hadn't ridden to Cerro and slipped that gun through the window last night, we'd still be waiting for old Fat Guts to hang us like he promised. You ain't treating 'em right, Jake.'

They swung off the road toward the river and a moment later disappeared into the cottonwoods along the east bank. They rode slowly through the trees, for the water was high and they couldn't follow the path along the edge of the stream as they ordinarily would have done.

Presently Jake said, 'I don't savvy you, Bud. What difference does it make whether we treat a bastard like Joe Tucker right or not? If he had the guts to take that dinero off the stage, you can bet he'd do it, but instead of that, he busts us out of jail so we'll take the chance of Reno Moore plugging us, then he claims a third of what we make. To hell with him.'

'And I don't savvy you,' Bud shot back. 'You kept your bargain with him three years ago when he told us about the dinero Kelsey had hid in his yard. We beef Kelsey and his wife just like Tucker wants and we give him a

44

third. Then, like damn fools, we let the girl stay alive because Tucker says to. If she ever sees us again, she'll identify us.'

'No she won't. It don't make no difference anyhow. I don't do nothing without good reason, which same you ought to know. Three years ago we needed friends like Joe Tucker. Now we don't because we're leaving the country. Fifty thousand dollars will buy us a right good hacienda in Sonora or Durango if we keep going. Or did you forget we was retiring?'

'Hell no, I didn't forget,' Bud said, 'but I don't like the notion of being so close to the Girard girl. I said then and I still say we should have plugged her.'

No use to argue, Jake thought. Bud never wanted to leave a witness. Maybe it was a good principle at times, but more often than not, too much killing was worse than not enough. He glanced at Bud, then lowered his head as he ducked under a cottonwood limb.

The trouble with Bud was that sooner or later he'd kill after they reached Mexico regardless of the need for it and they'd have to run again. He was like a man who drank too much or couldn't keep away from a poker table. In his way Bud was sick and therefore dangerous. The only way to be safe was to put a bullet into his back and ride on alone. After this job was done, of course. As much as Jake hated killing, it was the logical thing to do, and Jake prided himself on being logical.

They reached the road and stopped, Jake staring through the rain at the river where the bridge should be. He rubbed a wet hand across his eyes and leaned forward in the saddle. Sure, this was where the bridge should be. The approaches on both sides were exactly where Jake had remembered them, but there simply wasn't any bridge over the dirty, pounding water.

Bud began to curse. Then he said, 'I've had a bad feeling about this job right from the . . .'

'Shut up, damn it,' Jake said. 'I don't want to hear no more of that crazy talk. The stage ain't going to Gold City tonight. It'll be right there at the roadhouse. If it's there, the money's there, so we'll ride in and get it.'

'Have you gone completely crazy?' Bud demanded. 'I suppose we'll go to the door and say please, stage driver, can we rob you of the money?'

'You keep on being funny and I'll knock you pizzle end up right out of your saddle,' Jake said. 'Listen now and listen good. We'll stay in the trees till dark, then we'll ride up to the house and say we was headed for Gold City but the bridge is out, so we want supper and a room. If we wait it out we'll find the dinero, then we'll take it and ride. We ain't passing this up. Savvy that?'

'I savvy you're a knot-headed fool,' Bud burst out. 'Go in there and let the girl look at us? Now maybe you can see why we should have...'

'No, we done right letting her live. She didn't get a good look at us. Besides, you've growed up and I've got a beard. I didn't have one then. She'll think we're just a couple of pilgrims heading for a job in the mines in Gold City.'

Bud knew this meant death as certainly as if he had taken his .45 and put the muzzle to his forehead and pulled the trigger. He tried to meet his brother's stare, tried to make his right hand draw his gun and cut Jake down where he sat his saddle no more than five feet away. He was faster than Jake, a lot faster. He knew he could do it, but in the end he looked away. Obeying Jake had become a habit; he couldn't break it now.

'All right,' he said sullenly. 'We'll play it your way.'

'You're damned right we will,' Jake said, and riding back into the cottonwoods, motioned for Bud to follow.

## CHAPTER SIX

Every time Glen was here when the stage came in, he marveled at the manner in which

Susan met the passengers, smiling and shaking hands with them at the door and introducing herself if she didn't know them. She was always pleasant and friendly regardless of what her own problems and troubles were. The passengers were impressed and pleased, for this was not the reception they usually received at a meal stop.

Tonight there were four. Glen knew two of them, the rancher Sam Kerwin and a Baptist preacher named Harlan Wells, an old man who had not held a pulpit for several years. Instead, he was devoting his life to what he called 'The Home,' an orphanage for children of miners.

The need was great, as Glen, who had spent much of his life in the mining country, well knew. He regularly gave sizable contributions to Wells, but he was aware that most of the businessmen in Gold City didn't. He often wondered how Wells was able to keep the Home going.

The third passenger was a woman in her thirties, brown-haired and blue-eyed, and rather pretty. She was introduced to Glen by Susan as Mrs. Lola Avery who was to teach the lower grades in the Gold City school. The fourth was her son Frosty, a freckled-faced kid about twelve. Glen held his hand out to the boy, but Frosty ignored it, his lower lip jutting out belligerently.

'He needs a shave, Mamma,' Frosty said shrilly. 'Why don't he shave?'

'Hush,' Mrs. Avery said reprovingly, and smiled at Glen. 'He's tired. We rode the stage from Grand Junction to Cerro and from Cerro out here in all that terrible storm.'

Glen turned away, wondering how a woman could handle a roomful of children if she couldn't teach manners to her own son. Bronc Kline and Reno Moore, still carrying the box, were behind Glen. Kline winked, and Moore said out of the corner of his mouth, 'Watch him. He's a holy terror.'

'Hang your coats in the hall and come on into the dining room,' Susan said. 'Supper's ready.'

'You suppose she's got anything fit to eat?' Frosty asked. 'I'm hungry.'

'Of course she has, darling,' Mrs. Avery said as she hung his dripping coat on the hall tree. 'Let's go see.'

They followed Susan into the dining room as Molly brought a heaping plate of biscuits from the kitchen and set it on the table. She was turning toward the kitchen when Frosty said, 'Them biscuits look like rocks, don't they, Mamma?'

Molly whirled back to stare at him, her big hands on her hips. She opened her mouth, but before she could say anything, Susan interrupted with, 'Her biscuits are very good,

Frosty. Molly, fetch the coffee.'

Frosty sat down before anyone else and immediately took a biscuit from the plate and broke it open. He reached for the dish of apple jelly and spooned out a liberal helping. Moore and Kline set the box next to the wall behind their chairs, grunting as if it was very heavy.

'What's in it, Mr. Moore?' Frosty asked around a mouthful of biscuit and jelly.

'Gold,' Reno Moore said. 'Fifty thousand dollars in gold.' He nodded at Susan. 'If you'll excuse me a minute, there's something else I want to fetch in from the coach.'

Molly came in with the coffee pot as the others sat down. She was in time to see Frosty take another biscuit from the plate. She asked, 'Well, how do you like my rocks, sonny?'

'They're all right,' he said in a belittling tone as he reached for the jelly.

From past experience Glen knew that the one thing Molly was vain about was her cooking. Amused, he watched her begin to swell like an inflated balloon, her hands half raised as if she was going to grab him by the shoulders and shake his teeth loose. Susan stopped her with, 'I guess the number he eats is proof of how well he likes them, Molly. Don't pour Reno's coffee yet. He went back to the coach for something.'

Grumbling, Molly disappeared into the

kitchen. Glen said, 'You had a narrow escape right then, son. You'd do better to kick a bear in the teeth than insult Molly's cooking.'

'I didn't insult her old cooking,' Frosty muttered. 'I just said her biscuits were all right.'

Susan shook her head at Glen. For a time no one said anything as the food was passed. Presently Moore returned with a bulging gunny sack in his hand. He sat down beside Kline, dropping the sack on the floor beside him.

'Sorry I'm late,' Moore said. 'Now I'm going to be a lot of bother. Pass everything.'

'You want everything passed just when we get into position to eat,' Kline grumbled.

'Can't help it,' Moore said. 'I'm perishing from hunger.'

'Feed the man,' Molly said as she came back from the kitchen with the coffee pot. 'He can stow away more grub for a little man than anybody I ever seen.'

'I'm not a little man,' Moore protested. 'I can lick any man here.'

Everyone laughed but Frosty who regarded him speculatively. He said, 'I don't believe it. You can't lick him.' He pointed at Kline. 'Or him.' He aimed a finger at Glen. 'I ain't sure you can even lick him.' He jerked a thumb in Sam Kerwin's direction. 'Let's see you take 'em on after supper.'

51

'He'd go through 'em like a buzz saw tearing through a bunch of tough knots,' Molly said. 'One day I seen a bear chasing him till he was so tired he couldn't run no more, so he stopped and turned around. There came the bear, his mouth open and droolin' for a bite of Moore meat, but he didn't get none. Reno just ran his arm down the bear's throat, grabbed him by the tail and turned him inside out. He gave the bear a kick and started him running the other way.'

Frosty gave her a scornful look. 'You expect me to believe that hogwash?'

Molly stood behind him, the coffee pot in one hand, the other hand raised so she could swipe him across the side of the head. 'You calling me a liar, sonny?'

'Molly,' Susan cried, 'bring in some more biscuits.'

Frosty sat motionless. He swallowed, choked, and finally said, 'No ma'am.'

'A polite boy you got there, Mrs. Avery,' Molly said, and stalked out of the room.

'When she comes back, you'd better tell her how good her biscuits are,' Glen said.

'Aw, she wouldn't have hit me,' Frosty said loudly. 'She wouldn't have dared.'

'Dared?' Moore laughed. 'Sonny, I know for a fact that Molly Tucker ain't afraid of nothing in this world.'

'Frosty,' Mrs. Avery said worriedly, 'you should eat something besides biscuits. The

52

roast is real good, and the gravy and potatoes...'

'I ain't hungry,' Frosty said, and looked around in surprise when everyone laughed.

Molly returned with another plate of biscuits. 'Well, little man, how do you like my rocks by now?'

Frosty swallowed, glanced at Moore to see if he had been joking, and apparently decided he wasn't. 'They're good, ma'am,' he said. 'Awful good.'

Even Mrs. Avery contributed to the general laughter, but Frosty didn't so much as grin. He reached for a biscuit with one hand and the jelly with the other.

'Manners are important, young man,' Harlan Wells said. 'I try to teach them to my family all the time. I have eleven boys and three girls, and I must admit that proper manners do not come easy to any of them.'

'I'd like to visit your Home,' Susan said. 'From all I've heard, you do a wonderful job with those children.'

'He does,' Glen said. 'I've been there.'

'Thank you.' Wells stared at his plate, overcome by emotion for a moment. Recovering his self control, he looked at Glen. 'But right now it looks as if I'll lose the Home. Unless the good Lord intervenes, I will.'

Surprised, Glen said, 'I didn't think it was that bad. Everyone knows what you're

53

doing.'

'They know,' Wells agreed bitterly, 'but you're the only businessman in Gold City who makes a regular contribution of any size to the Home. I had to mortgage the property to the bank some time ago. I haven't been able to pay the interest, so last week, Bill Buckner came to me and said he would not extend my time. I have just three days to raise the money.'

'It's a damned shame,' Sam Kerwin said. 'Buckner ain't that hard up.'

'Indeed he isn't,' Wells said, 'but I have yet to meet a banker who doesn't have ice water in his veins. Talk about your Simon Legrees and Shylocks. The terrible part of it is that when you consider the amount of money that is spent in Gold City every day for liquor, or goes over the gaming tables...'

'You're talking right at me, Harlan,' Glen said. 'My bar makes more money than my hotel does. But quit worrying. I'll talk to Buckner when I get back.'

'I didn't mean you, Glen,' Wells said quickly. 'I said you were the one man...'

'But I'm guilty just the same,' Glen said. 'I tell you I'll fix it if I have to take a club to Buckner.'

'Nobody will fix it if we don't...' Kline stopped so suddenly that Glen suspected he'd received a nudge from Moore's elbow. 'I mean, if old Bill Buckner's head is as hard as I think it is, you couldn't soften it with a club.'

'Then I'll use something besides a club,' Glen said.

A moment later everyone was through eating, with even Frosty staring at the lone biscuit on the plate with a jaundiced eye. Tucker had not come in to eat. Molly would probably feed him in the kitchen. He didn't want to show his battered face, Glen thought, and was glad he hadn't come to the table. His appearance would have forced an explanation that would not have been easily made.

'Might as well give you folks the bad news now,' Kline said. 'I thought I'd wait till we got our stomachs full. What with the storm and all, I guess none of us feel real good. The storm raised Cain all around. It took the bridge out over the Sundown River, so we'll have to spend the night here.'

The passengers stared at him, stupefied. Then Frosty demanded, 'You mean we've got to stay all night in this old firetrap?'

'You'll find the beds quite comfortable,' Susan said coldly.

'It isn't that,' Mrs. Avery said. 'You see, we're expected in Gold City tonight. I wanted to start looking for a place to live. I've just got to have everything fixed before school starts. I won't have time afterward.'

'I have to raise that money for Buckner,'

Harlan Wells said plaintively. 'Even with your help, Glen, it will take all the time we have.'

'I know,' Glen said. 'I hate it as bad as any of you, but there's nothing we can do. I've seen the river.'

'I suppose you have to be back tonight, too, Sam,' Kline said.

Kerwin was staring at his plate as if he didn't see it. Now he looked at Kline. 'I sure do. I've got just one man and I shouldn't have left him alone.'

'I've got mail to go through.' Kline nodded at the box on the floor. 'And that money has to be in Gold City before Monday morning, but I'm not sure we can even get a horse across the river tomorrow. Well, we're all in the same boat.' He pushed back his chair and got up. 'Glen, give me a hand with the luggage, will you?'

'What's in your sack, Mr. Moore?' Frosty asked.

'Goober feathers,' Moore said with a straight face.

'What's goober feathers?'

'They come off sidehill gougers,' Moore said. 'They're very expensive because it's hard to find sidehill gougers.'

'Can I see them?'

'Hell, no!' Moore said as he rose from the table. 'I don't let nobody look at my goober feathers.'

Kline shot him a worried glance, then said, 'Come on, Glen,' and left the dining room.

## CHAPTER SEVEN

Glen had taken his slicker off the hall tree and was putting it on when he heard a shouted curse from the dining room, pounding feet from the dining room into the parlor, and Frosty's voice screeching, 'I just wanted to see what a goober feather looked like.'

'What do you suppose the little varmint has done now?' Kline groaned.

Glen ran into the parlor, Kline a step behind him. Reno Moore had Frosty by the nape of the neck, his face livid with fury. His right hand was lifted to slap the boy, but before he delivered the blow, Mrs. Avery screamed and clutched his upraised arm with both hands.

'You're not going to hit Frosty,' Mrs. Avery yelled. 'What kind of a beast are you, hitting an innocent little boy?'

'Innocent?' Moore released Frosty and yanked free from Mrs. Avery's grip. Stooping, he picked up the sack that Frosty had dropped, then straightened and faced Mrs. Avery. 'Maybe you'd better get it through your head that everybody is an innocent lamb compared to that little demon of yours.'

Frosty retreated to stand behind his mother. He poked his head around her to glare at Moore. 'I never hurt nothing. I told you I just wanted to see a goober feather.'

'There isn't such a thing, honey.' Mrs. Avery waggled a finger under Moore's nose. 'If you hadn't told a lie like that to him, he wouldn't have taken the sack. You ought to be ashamed of yourself, a big man like you...'

'Yes ma'am,' Moore said. 'I am ashamed that I didn't knock his head off. Maybe the rest of us would have some peace around here if I had.'

Susan, Molly, Sam Kerwin, and Harlan Wells were standing in the dining room doorway, Molly laughing so hard she had to sit down, but no one else seemed to find any humor in the situation. Susan came on into the parlor and took Mrs. Avery's arm. 'I'll show you your room. I think you and Frosty will feel better after a night's sleep.'

'I ain't sleepy,' Frosty said sullenly, 'and I won't be shut up in no room before it's even dark. I'm not a baby.'

'You sure act like one,' Moore said. 'Bronc, wouldn't surprise me none if he made off with that fifty thousand dollars in there. Only thing is I don't think he can lift the box.'

Furious, Mrs. Avery took two quick steps and slapped Moore across the face. 'Don't call Frosty a thief. If it wasn't for those lies about goober feathers, this wouldn't have happened.'

'I think she's right,' Kline said. 'You might just as well show them what's in the sack, Reno. I suppose it's natural for the kid to be curious about goober feathers.'

Affronted, Moore said, 'What the hell, Bronc? This was your...'

'Show the boy what's in the sack, Reno,' Kline said.

Moore chewed on his lower lip a moment, glaring at Kline, then he reluctantly nodded as if finally understanding the stage driver's line of thinking.

'It's just some of my dirty clothes,' he said. 'There's a woman in Gold City who does real good with my shirts. I let a bunch of 'em gather up in Cerro, then I stuff 'em into this sack and fetch 'em along to Gold City.' He untied the string and opening the sack, let Frosty see a wadded-up shirt. 'I didn't want nobody looking at my dirty clothes, or even knowing I was toting 'em around. That's why I called 'em goober feathers.'

'A great pride, I must say,' Mrs. Avery said scornfully.

'You might say I am proud, Mrs. Avery,' Moore said, 'but I ain't too proud to lay a hand on the backside of that brat of yours if he bothers anything of mine again.'

'You touch him once more,' Mrs. Avery said, 'just once more, and I'll pull every one of your red hairs out by the roots.'

'Mr. Kline, please bring in the luggage,' Susan said sharply. 'Mrs. Avery, I'll show you and Frosty your room.'

Kline wheeled and strode into the hall and on through the door. Glen caught up with him and they walked through the rain to the coach, the mud squishing under their boots. Kline said, 'That damned Reno owns a hair-trigger temper. The brat got under our hide the minute he showed up with his ma this morning, but Reno's got no business letting it get the best of him. Now I suppose everybody is wondering what's in the sack besides shirts.'

'I doubt that anybody but me thought about it,' Glen said. 'Is all the money in the sack?'

'Every cent,' Kline answered. 'We've got rocks in the box. The money is all in greenbacks, but we talk about it being gold.'

Kline lifted four valises from the boot of the coach and handed them down to Glen. 'Damned near dark,' he grumbled. 'Shouldn't be for another hour yet.' He swung down and went on, 'You see, the word got out in Cerro about the money. I dunno how, but it did. It ain't easy to raise that much dinero on short order, so when

Buckner wired for it, there was a lot of scurrying to get it. Anyhow, as we was loading up, there was the usual crowd hanging around and some joshing about how we'd better be careful, carrying that much cash. Ordinarily we'd have left it right in the box, but we got to talking after we heard about the Brittons getting out. Maybe they don't know about the money, but then, maybe they do, so Reno and me figured they'd take the box and wouldn't pay no attention to a plain old gunny sack.'

'If the money's in greenbacks, it'd be soaked by now,' Glen said.

'No, we wrapped it in a slicker and shoved it in the bottom of the sack,' Kline said, 'then we threw several dirty shirts on top so if anybody started pawing through them, they'd decide that's all there was.'

'Why didn't Reno just toss the sack down and not say anything?' Glen asked. 'I mean when he came in for supper. It was the gab about the goober feathers that started the ruckus.'

'Well, we thought it was better to make a fuss about the box and the amount of money that was in it,' Kline said, 'seeing as the talk was going around anyhow. So then we couldn't leave the sack in the coach, but it was bound to look funny if Reno went out into the rain a second time and fetched it in. That's why we decided to josh about the goober feathers, then we'd mention the laundry if we had to. I still think it would have been all right and nobody would have thought anything about it if it hadn't been for the damned kid.'

Glen picked up two valises. 'Let's get these inside,' he said. 'There's something in the barn I want to show you if Tucker isn't out there.'

They sloshed back through the mud to the house and set the valises in the hall, Glen calling to Susan that they were there, then they walked to the barn. Glen still wasn't sure that Kline and Moore had been right in the way they had handled the money, but now it was a case of hindsight and he was in no position to criticize.

If he had been in the shoes of either man, he might have done the same thing. He had heard of many instances of large sums being transported through dangerous, outlaw-infested country, and being brought safely to their destination by guile. On the other hand, he had known of other cases where strongboxes and locks and armed guards had not been able to prevent a holdup. The scheme was a good one and it still might work.

He opened the barn door and went in. Here it was too dark to see more than a few feet ahead of him. He said in a low tone, 'Keep your voice down. Tucker may be around here somewhere.'

He struck a match, found a lantern hanging from a nail just inside the door, and jacking up the chimney, touched the flame to the wick and eased the chimney down. He walked along the runway, calling, 'Tucker.'

No one answered. He moved on to the end of the runway looking in each stall, but finding no one, he went back to the stall that held Matt Girard's horse. He asked, 'You know this bay, Bronc?'

Kline took the lantern and going into the stall, looked the animal over. He stepped back and handed the lantern to Glen. 'Yeah, I know him. Five horses were stolen from the corral back of the livery stable in Cerro early this morning. Five men broke out of jail, so we naturally figured they got the horses. This bay is one of 'em.' He looked at Glen, his forehead creased by lines of worry. 'Now are you telling me that one of the Brittons rode him in here?'

'No, Matt Girard did,' Glen answered. 'Rode him in this afternoon during the worst of the storm. He's in the house now. Sue's trying to keep him hid because Tucker said he'd kill Matt if he showed up here again. Now maybe Matt's telling the truth when he said he was just trying to get away and had to come here, but there's a chance he's in the scheme with the Britton boys. Maybe he aims to throw a gun on us when the time's

63

right and pull out with the money.'

'Hell no,' Kline said. 'Matt don't have the guts. Besides, he wouldn't be here if he had any such notion. He didn't know the bridge was out. Neither did the Brittons, so if he was in on a deal with 'em, he'd go to wherever they planned to hold the stage up.'

'Sure,' Glen said in disgust. 'I didn't think of that. It's just that I don't trust Matt and I don't trust Joe Tucker, and I'm jumpy with that much money in the house.' He walked back to the door, and blowing out the lantern, hung it up. 'How long had Matt been in the jug?'

'Oh, a couple of weeks. Why?'

'What was he in for?'

'Breaking into a saloon and stealing a keg of whisky.'

They returned to the house, Glen wondering why Matt had lied. Maybe it didn't mean anything because he lied more often than he told the truth. He never seemed to need a reason.

'Well, what's Matt got to do with this?' Kline demanded.

'Nothing, I guess,' Glen said, 'but I'll have another talk with him. If he was in the jail with the Brittons for two weeks, he must have heard them talking.'

'Yeah, he probably did,' Kline said. 'You know how that Cerro jail is, a big cell on one side of the corridor and a couple of small ones on the other side. Jake and Bud Britton were in the small cells, and Matt and the rest were in the big one. The other two with Matt were just drunks who would have been out in a day or two, but Matt had a thirty-day sentence. I figure you're barking up the wrong tree, though. The Brittons ain't the kind who need help when it comes to holding up a stage, and they wouldn't take a man like Matt if they did.'

Glen sighed. 'I guess not, but I'm still going to talk to him. I'm damned tired of hearing his lies.'

## CHAPTER EIGHT

The rain had almost stopped when Glen and Bronc Kline cleaned their boots on the scraper, just an annoying drizzle that would probably keep up all night. Thunder still rumbled from the top of Storm Mountain with lightning playing among the peaks to the west and north.

'That river's going to be hell to cross in the morning,' Glen said.

'Sure will,' Kline agreed, 'but we've got to do it.'

'Bill Buckner's going to have a long wait at the stage depot tonight,' Glen said.

'By morning he'll have a tizzy,' Kline

laughed softly. 'Probably figure he's lost both the bank and the fifty thousand dollars. Well, I'd have felt sorry for him if I hadn't heard what the preacher said.'

They went in, closing the door behind them, and hung their hats and slickers on the hall tree. 'Funny thing,' Glen said. 'I thought Buckner was a reasonably decent man. Just goes to prove you can't...'

'I'll kill that kid,' Molly screamed from the kitchen. 'So help me, I'll skin him alive.'

Glen groaned. 'Now what are they chasing him for?'

They ran into the dining room to see Frosty circle the long table, Molly right behind him and losing ground. The boy apparently aimed to go up the stairs, but Reno Moore who had been sitting beside the gunny sack and the strongbox with his Winchester across his lap jumped up and stood at the foot of the stairs.

'I'll get him, Molly,' Moore shouted.

But Frosty was more agile than either of them. When he saw that the stairs were blocked, he dropped to his hands and knees and, scooting under the table, ran toward the kitchen.

'Susie, he's going back,' Molly yelled. 'Grab him. Damn it, grab him.'

Mrs. Avery had apparently been getting ready for bed. Now she raced down the stairs in her nightgown, pulling a maroon robe hastily around her and tying the cord as she ran, hitting every other step and stumbling and almost falling before she reached the foot.

'Don't you touch him,' Mrs. Avery screamed. 'Don't you lay a hand on him.'

Susan rushed out of the pantry in time to see Frosty run into the kitchen from the dining room. He slammed the swinging door behind him, catching Molly in the face and bringing a howl of pain from her. Frosty apparently intended to go out through the back door, but now Susan had that exit blocked, so he dived for the door into her bedroom.

Glen shoved Molly out of the way and pushed the swinging door aside in time to see Frosty charge out of Susan's bedroom, yelling, 'There's a man in there.'

He ran headlong into Glen's arms. He held the boy until he quit struggling and stood panting beside Glen who looked past him at Susan. 'What did he do this time?'

'I don't know,' she said. 'I was in the pantry when Reno hollered for Molly and she started yelling she'd skin him alive.'

'I heard that.' Glen turned the boy so he faced him, his hands gripping both shoulders. 'What did you do?'

'Nothing.' The boy stared sullenly at the floor. 'I don't have to do nothing for them to start chasing me. That old woman who made the biscuits was hollering she was going to kill me, so I ran.'

'That was natural enough,' Glen grinned. 'Yes, sir, I'd have run, too.'

Molly pushed the swinging door back and propped it open. She stood with one hand on her nose, drops of blood showing between her fingers. Kline followed, holding Mrs. Avery by an arm. Her face was bright red, her eyes gleaming with fury, and Glen, looking at her, decided that a mother wildcat protecting her young would be no more fierce than Mrs. Avery was at that moment.

'I want to know why you keep picking on my boy?' Mrs. Avery demanded shrilly. 'You've been making him miserable from the minute we got here.'

'Who's been making who miserable around here?' Molly demanded. 'We've had kids here before, all ages and shapes of 'em. We've had Indians who had jumped their reservation in Utah and stopped here for meals. We've had outlaws, but by jings, we've never had anything to compare to this infernal brat.'

'What did he do?' Susan asked.

'Yes, I'd like to know what he could possibly have done that would make a grown woman like you want to kill a child,' Mrs. Avery said in the same high voice.

'Do?' Molly cried. 'Well, I'll tell you what he done. He was supposed to stay upstairs with you, but he sneaked back into the dining room. Reno let out a holler. This ... this little devil was up on the table pouring salt from the shaker into the sugar bowl.'

'Frosty, you didn't do that,' Mrs. Avery said. 'Tell mother you didn't.'

'I did,' Frosty admitted, looking at the floor. 'Just a little.'

'Why?' Mrs. Avery demanded. 'Why would you do a thing like that?'

Frosty wiggled and shifted his weight nervously from one foot to the other. Finally he said, 'Well, I thought it would be fun to see how everybody looked in the morning when they put sugar into their coffee.' He pointed at Molly. 'I'll bet she'd sour milk just looking at it after she tasted the coffee.'

In spite of anything he could do, Glen started to laugh. Kline turned and walked back into the dining room where he could laugh in private, and even Susan smiled, but Molly's harsh expression did not soften and Mrs. Avery was more horrified than amused.

'I'm ashamed of you,' Mrs. Avery said. 'You tell them you're sorry.'

'I sure am,' Frosty said. 'I'm doggone sorry that old redheaded goat with the Winchester saw me. I had my back to him and I didn't think he'd know what I was doing.'

Glen pushed the boy toward his mother. 'You'd better keep him in your room, Mrs.

Avery. Next time Molly might catch him.'

'We've had enough of his pranks,' Susan said. 'If you don't keep him in your room and out of trouble, I'll lock him up where I know he can't get into mischief.'

Mrs. Avery whirled and taking Frosty by the hand, led him out of the kitchen. Molly returned to the pan where she had been washing dishes, an occasional drop of blood still falling from her nose. Susan looked at her broad back and shook her head, then winked at Glen.

'Heaven deliver us from having such a child,' she whispered, and returned to the pantry.

Glen waited until he was sure he wouldn't laugh in front of Molly, then he turned to her. 'Where's Joe?'

She looked at him sourly. 'You laugh at the capers of that little fiend and then you have the gall to come and talk to me.'

'Yes ma'am,' Glen said. 'I've got gall, all right, but you know, it would have been funny in the morning when we used that sugar.'

Molly said, 'Humpf,' and kept on washing dishes, refusing to look at Glen.

'Where's Joe?'

'He's in our room in bed,' she snapped. 'I suppose you want to beat him some more.'

'It would be a pleasure,' Glen said.

'You done a good job already,' Molly said

angrily. 'You busted his nose and you cut his lip. He hurts.'

'I hurt where he nailed me a couple of times,' Glen said. 'It just doesn't show. Does he know yet he's going to get fired?'

'No. Susan won't tell him till she finds another man.'

'Why do you go on living with him?' Glen asked. 'You deserve a better husband.'

'Oh, he's a good husband,' Molly said. 'He hardly ever hits me.'

Glen turned away and went into Susan's bedroom. He had known many women who lived with men who were no good, some even vicious, and he'd heard a variety of reasons for their staying together, but Molly's explanation was the stupidest. If she'd go after Joe the way she had Frosty, she might straighten him up, but she never would. That was the strange part of it.

'Who was the kid?' Matt asked. 'I heard all that hollering and running, then the boy comes in here, sees me and runs out slamming the door behind him, and the commotion breaks out again.'

'One of the passengers.' Glen looked at a tray on the floor that was filled with dirty dishes. 'Looks like you had your supper.'

Matt patted his stomach. 'Yes sir, I did. Sure better than the jail slop they gave us in Cerro.'

'I guess you had quite a few meals in that

71

jail,' Glen said. 'Two weeks make fourteen days. Three meals a day figures forty-two meals, doesn't it?'

Matt squinted at him, uncertain about how to answer, then he said, 'Yeah, guess that's right. I didn't count 'em.'

'With a thirty-day sentence, you had sixteen to go. That was a pretty stiff sentence for getting drunk, wasn't it?'

Matt kept on squinting at him, still uncertain how to answer. Finally he said, 'Yeah, I thought it was purty stiff.'

'But maybe you weren't drunk.'

'Well, I was,' Matt said. 'Sort of. I stole some whisky from the Belle Union. If I'd drank it, I'd of been drunk, wouldn't I?'

This seemed the same kind of reasoning that Glen had heard from Molly when she explained why she stayed with Joe Tucker. Glen said, 'Matt, seems to me that lying comes easier to you than telling the truth.'

'Why, I reckon it does,' Matt said amiably. 'Hell, them lies I told you didn't hurt nothing. I figured maybe Susan hadn't heard 'bout me being in jail and I didn't want her to. For stealing whisky, I mean, so I just let on I'd got drunk. I didn't want you to know, neither, with you gonna be my son-in-law and all.'

'All right,' Glen said. 'Now for once tell me the truth. You were in the same jail as the Britton boys were for two weeks. Just across the corridor from them. You must have heard them talk.'

'Sure they talked,' Matt said, 'but nothing of importance. Just about their robbings and such. They killed that stage driver, all right.'

Glen grabbed a fistful of his shirt and pulled him into a sitting position. 'Listen to me. We've got fifty thousand dollars in this house the stage was taking to Gold City. I suppose you didn't hear anything about that?'

'No, Glen, I sure didn't.'

'The Britton brothers are loose. They may come here after it. Sue may get killed if there's a fight. So can I. You, too.'

'They won't come here. They'd go to wherever they aimed to hold the stage up.'

'Yeah, but if it's on the other side of the river, they'll find out the bridge is gone, and they'll know the stage is here. Now if you heard anything about their plans...'

'I don't know nothing,' Matt howled. 'Just that they was aiming to head east out of Cerro. That's all they said.'

Glen let go of his shirt and Matt's head and shoulders dropped back to the bed. 'Did you ever do a decent thing, Matt? For Sue or anybody?'

For the first time since he had met Matt Girard, he saw an expression of shame come over the ugly, stubble-covered face. Matt said, 'No, Glen, reckon I never did.'

'You've eaten her meals, you've taken her money, you've traded worn-out old nags to her for good horses. Now you've got a chance...'

'Damn it, Glen, I don't know nothing.'

'Oh hell,' Glen said, and wheeled around and stalked out of the room, slamming the door behind him.


# CHAPTER NINE

Darkness came nearly an hour earlier than usual, the black clouds still hanging low, the cold drizzle continuing. Glen had built a fire in the parlor fireplace, and now he stood in front of it beside Bronc Kline, his hands extended toward the flames. He rubbed his hands on his pants, then shivered as he jammed them into his pockets. The chill, damp air had penetrated the house, the fire having little effect upon it.

Bronc Kline grinned as he asked, 'Nervous?'

'A little.'

'So'm I,' Kline said. 'Funny thing. I've been held up, shot at, wounded twice, and I've driven the stage a dozen times or more with some real tough hombres inside who were being taken to the Canon City pen, but I've never felt like this. Kind of like knowing lightning is gonna hit you, and you're just standing around waiting for it to do it.'

Glen nodded. 'That's about the way I...'

Outside a man yelled, 'Hello the house.'

Glen looked at Kline. 'Maybe that lightning you were talking about is getting ready.'

Glen stepped into the hall, and, opening the front door, slid through it and stood with his back to the wall. He asked, 'Who's there?' He could make out the vague shape of two mounted men in front of the house just beyond the finger of lamplight that fell through the doorway. The Britton boys wouldn't ride up boldly to the front door like this, Glen thought. But he didn't know. Maybe they would.

For a moment neither of the men answered Glen's question, then one of them said, 'I'm Alfred Vance. This is my brother Ted. We were headed for Gold City, but the damned bridge is out, so we're looking for supper and a room.'

Glen hesitated, the thought nagging his mind that for all he knew, these fellows could be the Britton boys as well as Alfred and Ted Vance. He had never seen either of the Brittons, and now that he thought about it, he couldn't remember having heard or read an adequate description of either. Then the notion struck him that if these men were the Britton boys, it might be better to have them inside the house than outside where they could move under cover of darkness.

'We've got a stage-load of people here,' Glen said, 'so we're pretty full, but we'll see you get supper. Maybe we can find some kind of bed for you.'

'We'd be beholden to you,' the man said. 'This is a hell of a night to be out in.'

'Put your horses in the barn,' Glen said. 'You'll find a lantern inside the door to your left.'

The men rode off into the darkness, Glen remaining where he was until he saw the lantern come to life in the barn. When he stepped back into the hall, Kline was waiting for him.

'Who'd they say they were?' Kline asked.

'Alfred and Ted Vance. Ever hear of them?'

'Yeah,' Kline answered. 'They've got a ten-cow spread back in the hills above Cerro. I've never seen 'em to know 'em, but from what I've heard, they're a couple of purty tough hands.'

'Would you know the Brittons if you saw them?' Glen asked.

'No, I sure wouldn't,' Kline admitted. 'They've been in jail in Cerro for quite a while, but I never had a look at 'em. I've seen reward dodgers with their pictures on 'em, but I couldn't identify 'em from that.'

Glen went back to the kitchen where

Susan and Molly were finishing the dishes. When Glen told them that two men were coming in for supper and a room if Susan had one for them, Molly snapped, 'This ain't a short-order house. You just tell those drifters to keep on riding.'

'No, Molly,' Susan said gently. 'Not on a night like this. We'll warm up something for them. Glen, they can have the small room clear in the back.'

As Glen turned toward the dining room, Molly said irritably, 'You're just an easy mark. If these yahoos want supper, they ought to be here at suppertime. I'm dog tired and my feet are killing me.'

'You go on to bed,' Susan said. 'I'll take care of it.'

'I'll help you,' Molly grumbled. 'I guess I ain't no tireder'n you are.'

Glen was surprised and a little shocked at Molly's attitude. He had seen her put herself out on more than one occasion for travelers who drifted in at odd hours, but tonight she acted as if she didn't want any more strangers around.

He wondered if Molly's attitude had anything to do with the fifty thousand dollars Reno Moore was guarding, then dismissed the question from his mind. He was entirely too jumpy. Molly was probably in a foul mood because of the antics of the kid Frosty. Maybe she had lived with Joe so long she was getting to be like him.

Glen dropped into a chair beside Moore. 'You going to sit here in the dining room all night?'

'For a while,' Moore answered. 'Then I'll take the gunny sack and go to bed. Bronc will spell me off watching the box. Maybe you'll take a turn at it afore morning.'

Glen nodded. 'Sure. I suppose you'll use your sack of goober feathers for a pillow.'

'That I will,' Moore said, 'and I'll be sleeping with my six shooter in my fist. If anybody comes into my room tonight, I'll plug him and then wake up and ask him who he is.'

Glen grinned. 'Guess it'll be healthy to stay out of your room.' He rolled a cigarette, then asked, 'Ever see the Britton boys?'

'Nope. I stay out of jails as much as I can. I sure didn't go into the Cerro calaboose just to see them bastards.'

'Ever hear what they look like?'

'Not much. They're young. Jake's maybe twenty-five or thirty. He wears a beard. Bud, he's 'bout twenty. Real slender.'

'Ever hear of Alfred or Ted Vance?'

Moore shrugged. 'Heard of 'em. That's all. I don't have no idea what they look like. Loners, from what I hear. They run a few cows and a few horses, and live off their neighbors' beef, so the talk is.'

'A lot of men do that,' Glen said.

The Vances came in then, stamping the mud off their boots in the hall and hanging up their hats and slickers. They stepped into the dining room, their eyes swinging quickly from Glen to Reno Moore who sat beside the strongbox, the sack containing the fifty thousand dollars lying on the floor beside it.

Glen rose and tossed his cigarette stub into a spittoon. He had his first good look at the men then, and he was shaken by the fact that they tallied with the meager description Moore had given him of the Britton brothers. The older and heavier-set man was about thirty, Glen judged, and he wore a black spade beard. The other one was younger, probably not over twenty, and was so slender he gave the appearance of being frail. His features were fine, almost feminine.

The older man turned his face from Moore to Glen. 'The grub 'bout ready?'

Glen rose. 'I'll tell the cook you're here.'

He stepped into the kitchen, hoping that Susan would not read his feelings on his face. He was scared. If these were the Britton boys, he had reason to be scared. The younger one particularly had the reputation of being a cold-blooded killer, a man who killed for the sake of killing. Gold City attracted tough hands, and Glen had held his own with the worst of them, but he had never been up against a man like young Bud Britton.

'They're here,' Glen told Susan.

She was working at the stove, her back to him. She said, 'I'll have it ready in a minute.'

He returned to the dining room, deciding that if there was going to be trouble, this was the time to force it into the open. Reno Moore was looking at him, waiting for him to make a move, and Bronc Kline was watching from the parlor.

'It'll be ready in a minute, she says,' Glen said. 'Do you men have any identification on you?'

The young one had been staring at the strongbox at Reno Moore's feet. Now he wheeled, his right hand splayed above the butt of his gun. He demanded, 'Why'n hell should we give you any identification?'

Glen took a deep breath. The man who called himself Ted Vance was staring at him with a kind of wicked intensity that Glen had never seen in another human being's eyes. He seemed to be waiting for the slightest motion or word that would give him an excuse to go for his gun.

'I'm not asking for any trouble,' Glen said. 'If you start it, you'll wind up on the wrong end of it. This is Reno Moore, the guard on the stage that's lying over here tonight.' Glen nodded at Kline who was standing in the doorway behind the two men. 'Bronc Kline is back of you. He's the driver. A fair hand with a gun, too, so just ease off and answer my question.'

The young one's gaze didn't waver and he didn't relax until his brother said, 'He's right, Ted. No sense of us getting boogery just because he's nosy.'

The man nodded at Glen. 'Mister, I don't go around with an affidavit in my pocket saying I'm Alfred Vance and this is my brother Ted. We own a little cow outfit on the other side of Cerro, and we was aiming to ride into Gold City and see if we could deliver some beef cattle at a better price than we can get in Cerro. We wouldn't be spending the night here if the damned bridge hadn't gone out.' He reached into his pants pocket and brought out a wallet that he tossed onto the table, the coins inside jingling as it struck. 'If that won't do, we'll just have to go unidentified.'

Glen picked the wallet up. On one side gold letters, ALF VANCE, had been stamped into the leather. Age and use had nearly obliterated the words, but Glen could make them out. He saw no reason to press the point now, although he wasn't convinced by the wallet that the man was Alfred Vance. On the other hand, the slender description that Reno Moore had given him of the Britton brothers didn't prove anything, either.

Glen tossed the wallet back to the man. 'All right,' he said. 'Here's your supper.

81

Sorry I bothered you.'

'You ought to be,' the young one said angrily. 'By God, we ain't in the habit of being called liars.'

Susan and Molly had brought in plates piled high with food and cups of steaming coffee and had placed them on the table. Susan said, 'We'll bring the bread...'

From the top of the stairs the boy Frosty called, 'Who are you?'

Glen whirled toward the stairs as the boy came bouncing down, a wicked grin on his freckled face. This was perfect, Glen thought angrily as he started toward the foot of the stairs. Frosty's talent for doing the wrong thing was all they needed to produce an explosion, as touchy as Ted Vance was.

'Get back to your room,' Glen ordered.

Frosty stopped before he reached the bottom of the stairs. 'You know what's in that box?' Glen lunged toward him, but before he could clap a hand over the boy's mouth, Frosty yelled, 'Fifty thousand dollars in gold.'

Glen grabbed the boy and carried him up the stairs, holding him at his side with his right arm, his left hand over Frosty's mouth. He heard young Vance's derisive laughter, heard him say, 'Fifty thousand dollars in gold! So that's why you're so damned particular about who we are.'

Glen went on, saying nothing and not

looking back. He thought: *The fat's in the fire now. Good.*

## CHAPTER TEN

Glen went along the upstairs hall, carrying the kicking boy under his right arm like a sack of grain, his left hand pressing hard against Frosty's mouth. Mrs. Avery, still wearing her nightgown and maroon robe, had been waiting for him at the head of the stairs.

She reached out and gripped Glen's right arm with both hands as she cried, 'What are you doing to him now?'

Grim-faced, Glen jerked free and stalked on past her. She trotted behind, her slippers slapping against the bare hall floor. 'Mr. Logan, will you answer me please?' she asked, her voice high and shrill. 'Frosty has suffered one indignity after another from the minute we got off the stage. Why is he suffering this?'

Glen strode into their room and dumped the boy on the bed. 'All right, you've had your fun, kid,' he said. 'Now tell me what your idea was?'

Frosty sat up on the edge of the bed, his lower lip protruding in the belligerent way he had. He didn't say a word. He just sat there,

83

his eyes locked defiantly with Glen's. Even when Glen raised a hand to slap him, the boy didn't cringe or shift his gaze.

Mrs. Avery was tugging frantically at Glen's threatening hand. 'Don't hit him. Tell me what he did. If he has to be punished, I'll do it.'

Glen dropped his hand. He turned to the woman who had stepped back, her eyes filled with a pathetic frustration that blunted the sharp edge of his anger.

'Mrs. Avery, have you ever punished this boy in his life?' Glen asked.

She stared at the floor. 'Not enough perhaps.' Then she raised her gaze to Glen's face. 'He's a good boy, Mr. Logan, but people pick on him. That's the trouble.'

'And why?' Glen demanded. 'I guess you wouldn't know. Well, I'll tell you. He provokes it. He's discourteous. He ignores the rights of others. He hasn't the slightest respect for his elders.' Glen motioned toward the boy. 'Look at him. I asked him a question. He didn't answer me. He just sits there. Mrs. Avery, if you can't discipline your own boy—if you can't even teach him ordinary courtesy, how do you expect to handle a roomful of school children?'

She sighed. 'I'll handle them. You see, it's different with Frosty. His father died when he was three years old. He's all I have left to love, Mr. Logan.' She took a long breath and

84

then said, 'He'll answer your question, but first tell me what he did.'

'He came downstairs and saw a couple of strange men sitting at the table,' Glen said. 'He yelled to them that there was fifty thousand dollars in gold in the box Reno Moore was guarding.'

'Well, we all knew it,' Mrs. Avery said. 'There surely wasn't any secret about it. We were all told when we were eating supper.'

'Just those of us who were eating supper,' Glen said. 'Not these men who came in late. Now I asked your boy what his idea was.'

'Tell him, darling,' Mrs. Avery said. 'I don't see any reason why it was worse to tell these men than anybody else, but maybe there is.'

'There's a plenty good reason,' Glen said angrily. 'Besides, he was told to stay in his room.'

'I got tired of sitting in this old room,' Frosty said resentfully. 'Nobody else has to stay in theirs. It's bad enough to have to stay overnight in a stinking old house like this without being made to stay in my room.'

'All right, you got tired of staying in your room,' Glen said. 'Why did you tell the men about the money?'

'I was mad at that old goat who's guarding it,' Frosty said. 'He helped the fat old woman who made the biscuits chase me all over the house.'

'You were mad at him,' Glen said, 'so you thought it would make him mad when you told the strangers about the money.'

'I guess so,' Frosty muttered. 'I guess I didn't figure out why I done it. I just saw the men at the table and I done it.'

'Did it, darling,' Mrs. Avery corrected. 'Not done it.'

'Mrs. Avery,' Glen said, 'you wanted to know why it was worse to tell these men about the money than it was to tell everyone at supper. All right, I'll answer that question. What Frosty did may cost us our lives. Mine and Reno Moore's and Bronc Kline's, all because your boy didn't stay in your room the way he was told.'

'Now Mr. Logan,' Mrs. Avery said, as if amused by what he had said. 'This is ridiculous. You mean to tell me that these two men may kill you, but none of us who were at the supper table were dangerous?'

'That's right,' Glen said. 'I knew everybody at the supper table except you and Frosty. I don't know these men, but we have reason to think that they are the Britton boys. Did you ever hear of them?'

Mrs. Avery sat down suddenly, a hand coming up to her throat. 'Yes, I have. They just broke out of the jail in Cerro, didn't they?'

'That's right,' Glen said. 'These men claim to be ranchers from the other side of

Cerro. They say they're headed for Gold City, but it's my guess they're the Brittons. We know they rode east when they left Cerro, so they probably circled the town and came this way to throw the sheriff off the trail. If the bridge had been in, the chances are they'd have kept on going, but when they saw they couldn't get across the river, they decided to spend the night here, the storm being what it is. If they hadn't found out about the money, they might have gone on without making any trouble, I suppose, but now they won't leave without it.'

'But Frosty didn't know,' Mrs. Avery protested.

'No, but if he'd done what he'd been told to do, it wouldn't have happened. I'm telling you all of this so you'll know it's a touchy situation. Human lives mean nothing to the Britton boys, yours, mine or Frosty's.' He paused, then added slowly, emphasizing each word, 'Now will you keep the kid in this room the rest of the night?'

'Yes, Mr. Logan.' Mrs. Avery turned to Frosty. 'You stay right here in the room.'

The boy's eyes were sharp with excitement. Glen doubted that he had heard a word his mother had told him. Glen said, 'Frosty, if you come downstairs again before morning or even leave this room, I'll take a strap to you. Savvy?'

'They're real live outlaws, ain't they?'

87

Frosty asked. 'I never saw one before, did I, Mamma?'

'No darling, I don't think you ever did.'

'Gee whiz, Mr. Logan, how many men do you suppose they've killed?'

'I don't know,' Glen answered. 'Now are you going to stay in this room till morning?'

'Oh, sure,' Frosty snickered. 'Say, I'll bet that old goat was mad when I hollered about the money.'

Glen swung on his heel and walked out of the room, closing the door behind him. No use, he thought, no use at all. He could threaten the boy until he was black in the face and it wouldn't do any good. If Frosty decided to leave the room, he'd do it, and his mother wouldn't lift a finger to stop him.

'Glen.' Harlan Wells stood in the doorway of his room, motioning for Glen to step inside. 'I want to talk to you a minute.'

Glen hesitated, knowing he should be downstairs, but there was a worried expression on the preacher's lined face. He was probably thinking about Bill Buckner, Glen decided, and the mortgage the banker held on Wells's Home. To brush the old man off brusquely and say he couldn't spare the time would hurt his feelings, and Harlan Wells had been hurt enough.

'Just for a minute,' Glen said, and stepped through the doorway into the preacher's room.

Wells followed and closed the door. He said, 'I'll admit I was eavesdropping. I consider myself an expert on boys, Glen. I mean tough, defiant boys who come from broken homes like Frosty has. I've worked with enough of them over the years so I should be an expert. It's been my experience that there aren't any bad boys. The problem is with us, the adults. With a boy like Frosty, we just have to be patient. It won't do any good to take a strap to him.'

Glen shook his head. 'Harlan, I guess you know more about boys than I do, but I know more about men like the Britton brothers than you do. If that's who we've got downstairs, we're in trouble. All of us. And why? Because Frosty's a blabbermouth. I say taking a strap to him is too good for him. Maybe you could do something for him if you had him, but his mother never will.'

'I know,' Wells said. 'That's often the trouble when a woman tries to raise a boy by herself.' He paused, troubled eyes on Glen. 'You really think these men are the Britton boys?'

'It's a good bet,' Glen said, 'but we don't know. We don't have anything to hold them on. If we're guessing wrong and take them prisoners, we're in a hell of a lot of trouble. All we can do is to keep our eyes open and wait for them to make a move.'

'You'd risk your life to keep them from

getting that money?' Wells asked.

'I've got to,' Glen said. 'That money has to go through to Gold City.'

'There's a great deal of evil in the world,' Wells said slowly, 'I'm more familiar with the kind of evil that a man like Bill Buckner does with the power that money has than I am with the violence the Brittons do with guns. I guess I'm selfish because you're the only chance I have of saving the Home. I don't want you to get yourself killed. The money isn't worth the life of a man like you, Glen.'

'The money is more important than you realize,' Glen said. 'The future of Gold City, and that includes you and your Home, depends on that money being in Gold City by Monday morning.'

Glen left the room, knowing that he had not brought any comfort to the preacher who did indeed know the evil that a man like Bill Buckner could do through and with his money. Maybe Harlan Wells could be helped later, but at the moment there were more pressing problems.

When Glen reached the dining room, he saw that Reno Moore was still sitting in his chair with his Winchester over his lap. Apparently neither man at the table had moved. Glen could not read the face of the older one, but the mocking malice in the eyes of the younger man was plain enough.

Susan brought two servings of apple pie from the kitchen. Glen, pausing at the foot of the stairs, could not mistake the expression of naked lust that appeared on the face of both men as their gazes followed her until she disappeared into the kitchen, then it was gone from the face of the older man, but it lingered in the cruel eyes of his brother even after he picked up his fork and began to eat.

Glen walked on into the parlor where Bronc Kline sat in front of the fireplace, his chair turned so he could watch the men at the table. Glen dropped into a chair beside him. He said in a low tone, 'How do you figure it?'

'If they ain't the Brittons,' Kline said softly, 'they're somebody else just as bad. That young one's a killing son of a bitch if I ever seen one. He's been spending that fifty thousand dollars ever since the kid hollered.'

Glen nodded, thinking it didn't make much difference whether these men were the Brittons or not. They were dangerous, whoever they were. The young one, if Glen was making the right judgment of him, would have the fifty thousand dollars before he left if it meant killing every person in the house.

There was a chance they could have been taken without trouble when they first came in, but they were alert now. The slightest threatening move on Glen's part would start

the ball rolling. He wasn't worried about
Molly Tucker, but with Susan and Mrs.
Avery in the house, he couldn't risk a blowup
if it could be avoided. There was nothing to
do but wait it out.

## CHAPTER ELEVEN

To Harlan Wells the ministry had been a
great illusion. For many reasons, most of
which were not his fault, he had learned that
it was difficult, perhaps impossible, to do the
good works he wanted to do and still stand
behind the pulpit two times on Sunday and
again on Wednesday night at prayer meeting
and to lead the choir every Thursday night at
its weekly practice.

A man had to be on the firing line if he
wanted to do anything that counted more
than mouthing sanctimonious clichés from
the pulpit. At least that was his conviction,
so he had retired from the active ministry
and had used his meager savings to buy a
two-story house with a mansard roof at the
head of the gulch above Gold City. Since
then he had devoted ten years of his life to
the mining camp's orphans.

Wells's work at the Home, and he insisted
on calling it that and would never accept the
word orphanage, was difficult and

exasperating but very satisfying. Some of the children he took in could pay for their room and board, but whether they could or not, he took them in.

He hired a woman who did the cooking and washing and ironing with the help of the older children. He did everything else, although unfortunately most of his time lately had been spent begging the businessmen of Gold City for financial help, which, except for Glen Logan's monthly contribution, had dwindled to a mere trickle.

He had reached the end of the line. Now, pacing back and forth in his room, he admitted it. He was over sixty, too old to go into the mines and earn a living. Even if he could, he wouldn't earn enough to keep the Home going.

Fourteen children were depending on him. The oldest ones understood the situation and knew why he had gone away. They were probably praying for him right now. But he had failed. Neither his prayers nor theirs had been answered.

He had prayed for success in this mission as he had never prayed for anything else in his life; he had read the Bible in hopes that the Divine Hand would point the way to him. Still, he had failed. He didn't know where the children would be sleeping a week from now. He did know it wouldn't take Bill Buckner that long to dispossess him.

This was like Little Nell pleading with the villain to give her father more time to save the old homestead, Wells thought bitterly as he stood staring at the dark, rain-splattered window.

The rain had almost stopped, but now he could hear it pounding on the roof again. Well, he wasn't Little Nell, but Bill Buckner was certainly the villain.

Gold City was filled with evil people: con men, gamblers, drunkards, gunslingers, pimps, and prostitutes. Wells knew many of them personally. He often went to the jail to talk to them. Sometimes he held services for them on Sunday mornings. Marshal Peter Doane took a cynical view of his visits, but he never discouraged Wells. 'Maybe you're doing some good, Parson,' Doane would say. 'I am sure of one thing. You can't do them bastards any harm.'

Sometimes Wells visited the girls in the cribs at the lower end of the gulch and talked to them. Some would curse him and call him the 'Come to Jesus man,' and others would laugh and invite him inside, pretending he was there on business, but he found a few who would listen. He had even persuaded several to quit.

This was the kind of evil which was recognized as evil, and yet, in Wells's opinion, it was a very small evil compared to the sins that Bill Buckner committed

94

through his bank and which were accepted by the community simply as sharp business practices. Buckner had never given a penny to the Home. As far as Wells knew, the banker did not contribute to any charity.

Buckner was a small man with thin lips, a sharp nose, and two black shoe buttons for eyes. He undoubtedly had a heart the size of a mustard seed. When Wells had gone to him asking about the mortgage, Buckner had been smilingly happy to oblige, promising that if Wells got behind, there would be no pressure to pay either the principal or the interest, but it had been an oral agreement with no witness. Buckner probably never intended to keep the promise. He was within his rights as far as the law was concerned, the rights of a man who considered the making of money the primary objective of life.

Suddenly the pressure which had been gathering in Wells for weeks broke his self-control and he shook his fist at the night-darkened window and he cursed Buckner with every oath he could think of. Then, out of breath, he stopped and sat down on the bed and wiped a sleeve across his sweaty face.

This was no good, he told himself. No good at all. Somehow it would work out if he had enough faith. He had to believe that. But the doubts crowded back into his mind. He had only three days left and so far he had completely failed.

He became aware of the talk from the Averys' room, of Frosty saying he wasn't sleepy and he was sick and tired of being penned up inside these dirty old walls, and of Mrs. Avery asking him to please stay in the room as Mr. Logan had asked him to.

Wells rose and, stepping into the hall, knocked on the door of the Averys' room. This wasn't any of his business, really, but he often butted into other people's business if he thought he could help, and this was a situation where he was sure he could.

When Mrs. Avery opened the door, Wells saw that she had been crying. Frosty sat on the edge of the bed, looking as defiant and belligerent as ever. Many a boy had come to the House with the same defiant attitude, but none had kept it very long.

'May I come in?' Wells asked.

Mrs. Avery nodded and stepped back, closing the door behind him. He said, 'I'm afraid I heard some of your conversation with your son, Mrs. Avery. The walls are pretty thin. I also heard the talk with Glen Logan when he was here.'

'Why don't you stick something in your ears?' Frosty demanded. 'It's our business what we talk about.'

'Indeed it is,' Wells agreed, 'but you see, boys are my business. Girls, too, but mostly it's boys that I deal with. Right now I have

96

fourteen children in the Home, of which eleven are boys.' He turned to Mrs. Avery. 'When you get to Gold City and start teaching, you're going to need help. It will take too much emotional energy to handle a schoolroom of children and then come home and take care of Frosty.'

She looked at him as if this same thought had been in her mind. She said, 'I don't know what I'll do. I've been worrying about it.'

'I have a suggestion,' Wells said. 'It's almost impossible to rent an apartment or house in Gold City. Or do you intend to buy?'

She shook her head. 'No. The money my husband left us is about gone. That's why I went to Normal School and why I'm going to teach. I didn't know anything else I could do.'

'My suggestion is that you find a place where you can room and board,' Wells said. 'I can help you. I know a number of places where I think you would be quite happy. We'll take Frosty into the Home. You could see him any time you wanted to, of course, but he'd live with us except when he's in school and he'd have boys of his own age to play with.'

'I'll think it over,' Mrs. Avery said. 'It sounds like a good idea.'

From the relief that flowed across her face,

Wells was convinced she would accept his suggestion. She was probably worn out from the trip. To make it worse, the trouble Frosty had been in from the time they had arrived had very likely brought her close to the breaking point.

'I won't do it,' Frosty said. 'I won't live in your old Home.'

Wells walked to the bed and looked down at the boy. 'If that is what your mother decides, that's what you'll do. It's the parent's job to make decisions.'

'I won't do it.' Frosty's mouth was drawn into a tight, stubborn line. 'You're like that old Logan. He says he'll take a strap to me if I leave this room. Well, I'm going to leave it. I'm going down and talk to those outlaws.'

'No, I won't take a strap to you,' Wells said gently. 'It won't be necessary. You see, boys have a way of disciplining members of their own group. They'll teach you manners. You'll find out that being rude and obnoxious the way you have been here will not get you the kind of attention you want.'

'I'm not rude and obnoxious,' Frosty said, meeting Wells's gaze. 'I just don't like being run over the way I have been around here.'

'Take a good, straight look at yourself, son,' Wells said. 'If you had shaken hands with Glen Logan instead of insulting him about needing a shave, if you hadn't insulted Molly Tucker's biscuits, if you hadn't put salt in the sugar, if you hadn't blabbed to the strangers about the fifty thousand dollars your reception here would have been quite different from what it has been. One of the best standards to measure a man is his willingness to accept responsibility for his own actions.'

Wells turned, nodded at Mrs. Avery, and left the room. It was not until he had closed his own door that he realized how stupid and perhaps cruel he had been to make the suggestion that he had to Mrs. Avery. After three days he wouldn't even have the Home.

He sat down on the edge of the bed, his head in his hands. He would do anything, he told himself, to get his hands on a few thousand dollars. That's all it would take to pay up his bills and get Bill Buckner off his neck. Anything, he told himself over and over. The end justified the means, and the end was worth doing anything for. He couldn't bear to lose ten years of work, the most important work he had ever done.

Then he thought of the fifty thousand dollars in the strongbox at the foot of the stairs. He had never seriously considered stealing anything before in his life, but he did now. The thought of stealing the money must have come directly from the devil. For the first time he was willing to give the devil some credit. The stage company could afford to lose the money, or the small part of it he would take.

Sure, it was wrong, but it was wrong for Bill Buckner to take the Home. The fact that the law would send Wells to prison for stealing money, but would condone what Buckner was doing seemed a minor detail. The question was how to do it without being caught. Obviously he would not accomplish anything for his children if he was sent to the pen at Canon City.

He got up and paced around the room again, thinking about how it could be done. He would have to wait until everyone except Reno Moore was asleep. Moore would probably try to stay awake all night, but later, sometime after midnight, he'd get drowsy. Possibly he would drop off into a light sleep right where he sat.

Wells could slip down the stairs and hit Moore from behind. He'd knock him out and then he'd open the box and take what he needed and get back quickly to his room. He had one big advantage over everyone else; he was the last man in the house who would be suspected.

He was excited, now that it was clear in his mind, so excited that he began breathing hard. He wouldn't be greedy, he told himself. That was the real sin, being greedy the way Bill Buckner was. Why, maybe Reno Moore wouldn't even count the money when he opened the box after he came to and saw that most of it was there. Moore wouldn't suspect that someone had taken just a little and left most of the money right there in the box when all of it could have been taken.

Then he realized that he had no weapon with which he could knock Moore out. The trick, of course, was to slip up behind the guard so he wouldn't be seen. But he couldn't use his fist. He had to have some kind of a club.

He looked around the room but there was nothing. He didn't have a gun. He had no way of getting one. He removed a shoe and thumped the heel against the palm of his left hand. No, that wouldn't do. He put the shoe back on, his gaze falling on the straight-backed chair. Sure, that was it.

He took hold of the back of the chair and laid it over on its side, then he brought his right foot down against a leg, snapping it off just below the seat. He picked the leg up and, jerking the splintered rung free from the leg tossed to the floor. Quickly he examined the leg. It was a solid piece of wood, well balanced, a lethal weapon in a killer's hand, but it wouldn't be in his. He wouldn't hit Moore that hard.

Kicking the rest of the chair under the bed, he tapped the leg against his left hand. It would do, he thought, it would do fine. Now it was just a question of waiting, and that wasn't going to be easy.

# CHAPTER TWELVE

Susan showed the Vance brothers their room, told them that breakfast would be ready at six o'clock, and went back downstairs. Reno Moore yawned loudly as she passed him. She stopped, smiling as she asked, 'Are you going to sit up all night, Reno?'

'Not if somebody comes to spell me off,' Moore said. 'Bronc promised he'd take a turn at it and Glen's going to spell him off.'

'Wouldn't it be easier to take the box upstairs to your bedroom?' Susan asked.

'Be easier,' he admitted. 'Likewise it would be dangerouser. If I went to bed, I'd go to sleep sure. Then it'd be simple enough for somebody to come in and knock me on the head or shoot me in the brisket and make off with the dinero.' He shook his head sourly. 'Trouble is, Susie, you just can't trust nobody when there's fifty thousand dollars in the house. I'll bet even old Harlan Wells is sitting up in his room figuring out how he can get his hands on this here gold.'

'Oh, not Harlan,' Susan said. 'Well, I'm going to bed. I hope you get some sleep.'

'So do I,' Moore said.

She blew out the lamp in the parlor. She left the bracket lamp in the hall and the one on the dining room table lighted, then went into the kitchen. Molly had put the dishes away and had gone to bed. Susan started toward the storeroom where she planned to sleep on the cot, then remembered that she had never gone after the dishes that had held her father's supper.

For a moment she hesitated. She didn't want to see Matt, and the dishes could certainly stay where they were until morning. But she knew she had better remind him that he was leaving before sunup. If he could, he'd go right on sleeping and be in bed tomorrow noon. Maybe he would anyhow, but at least she'd better remind him.

She found him stretched out on his back, his clasped hands under his head, his eyes wide open and staring at the ceiling. She was surprised to find him awake. 'I came in for the dishes,' she said, and stooping, picked the tray up.

'Sit down, honey,' he said. 'I've got something to tell you.'

She hesitated, thinking that not once since he had showed up the first time claiming he was her father had he ever said anything to her that was worth listening to. But maybe she would never see him again, and if she didn't listen, she would regret it.

She sat down on the edge of the bed, holding the tray of dirty dishes on her lap. She said, 'I'm terribly tired and I've got to go to bed, so I'll stay just a minute. What I really came in for was to tell you to have your horse saddled and be out of here before it's daylight. I don't think I can keep Joe Tucker from killing you if he finds you here.'

'Don't fret your purty head,' he said. 'I'll be out of here all right, though I sure don't know where I'll go. I aimed to ride to Gold City, but I can't make it with the bridge out.' He raised up on an elbow to look at her. 'You see, I stole that horse I was riding from a livery stable in Cerro. If I go back there, they'll hang me for horse stealing.'

This was the familiar pattern. First he promised the moon or anything else she wanted, then he'd start playing on her sympathy. It had always worked before, but it didn't tonight. He had played this tune too often. She stared at him, the stench from his unwashed body almost choking her.

To her at this moment he was just a repulsive old man. She couldn't remember why she had ever thought she owed him anything. The fact that he was her father was a matter of biology, not of emotion. She had put Glen off because of him; she would not do it again.

'You should have thought of that when you stole the horse,' she said, surprised by the harshness of her voice. She had not realized how much she despised him, how much she would have hated him if she had lost Glen because of him. 'You're getting out of here in the morning and you're not sweet-talking me into letting you stay. If Joe finds you here, he'll kill you.'

Matt sighed. 'It would solve a problem for you if he done it, honey, but I ain't staying. Glen loves you. You'd best marry him. He's a good boy. He'll make you a fine husband.'

'I know he will,' she said. 'I would have married him before now if it hadn't been for you. I've let you sponge off me, but I won't let you sponge off my husband. That's why you're leaving and you're not coming back.'

'No, I sure won't. Glen, he was in here a while ago and told me some things. He's real plain-spoken, Glen is. He asked me if I'd ever done a decent thing in my life, for you or anybody else. Well, it's kind of hard to come to my place in life and know you don't amount to a damn and nobody, not even your own daughter, cares what happens to you.'

'It won't work, so stop it,' she said. 'I'm not going to change my mind. I'll marry Glen just as soon as I can.'

She started to get up, but he reached out and gripped her arm and forced her to sit back on the bed. 'I ain't said what I was fixing to say,' he said. 'I always wanted you to think well of your mother, but now I reckon I'd better tell you about her, seeing as I'm leaving and not coming back. I know you've given me every chance in the world and I never took 'em. I kept right on sponging off of you, but you see, I done a decent thing once and I want you to know about it.'

She leaned away from him, but when he saw she was going to stay, he released his grip, his big hand dropping to his side again. She didn't want to hear what he was going to say. At best, it would be a distorted version of what had happened. Her mother had raised her and had given her a home; her mother had loved her and she had loved her mother. It wasn't right for Matt Girard to appear out of the past and destroy the image she had of her mother. Still she sat there, staring at him and listening.

'Your ma was real purty when we was married,' Matt said. 'Just about as purty as you are. Well, we homesteaded a piece of dry land out in the plains east of Denver. I was young and stout then, and I worked hard, but we was beat before we started. We hit a couple of dry years and prices was down for anything I had to sell. Then you was born and your ma near died having you. I couldn't get no doctor. Just me and a neighbor woman to help out. Something went wrong inside her and she couldn't have no more babies.

'After that your ma didn't act like she loved me any more. She wouldn't go to dances or school socials or nothing. She just sat in the house and rocked you and talked to you and sung to you, and acted like I wasn't even alive. Finally it got so we didn't have nothing to eat 'cept some knotty potatoes and beans and such. I didn't have no more credit in town, so I left her and you in that shack out there on the prairie with nothing around it but a crop of wheat I'd sowed. It came up and turned yaller and never headed out good 'cause we didn't get any rain at the right time. I won't never forget the last time I seen your ma, sitting on the porch in her rocking chair and rocking you. When I rode off, she didn't even wave at me.'

He stopped, staring past Susan as if he wasn't even aware she was in the room. She saw two tears roll down his face to be lost in the beard below his eyes. She had never known him to be touched by any sincere emotion before, nothing except the shallow self-pity which had been his way of getting her sympathy.

She knew that he lied as easily as he told the truth, but she had an uneasy feeling that what he had just told her was the truth. Her mother had seldom talked about Matt except to say that he had left her when Susan was a baby. Perhaps she had been ashamed she hadn't waited for him.

Matt stirred and wiped the back of a hand across his eyes. He went on, 'I got a job

107

mucking in a mine in Leadville. I didn't make much, but I sent back all I could spare to your ma and wrote to her to pay a little on the store bill. I never heard from her. Not once. Well, come spring I went back thinking I could get a crop in, but when I got there, she was gone. She'd just shut the door of our shack and walked off.

'I started asking around, and finally somebody told me the truth. She'd took you and run off with this Paul Kelsey. They'd been gone since October. Kelsey was a brother to a woman who lived on a ranch north of my place. He was visiting and got to smelling around your ma after I left, and I guess he talked her into going off with him.

'I found out your ma never paid off a nickel of the store bill. I didn't have nothing to live on, so I went to work for a neighbor. We had rain that spring and raised a crop, and I got my wages. I paid the store bill and stayed around all summer and fall, thinking I'd hear where Kelsey had took you and your ma. But I never did.

'Everybody was close-mouthed about what had happened. I guess they thought your ma was better off with Kelsey than with me. I didn't figure on getting her back, but I did want to see what you looked like.

'After that I went downhill, drifting around and drinking too much and never working very long anywhere. I didn't care about anything, but I did keep looking for Kelsey and your ma. I never got no trace of 'em till I heard they'd been murdered right here. I was in jail then, but I came as soon as I could.

'I won't never forget the first time I seen you, working in your yard in front of the house. When you stood up to look at me, it was like seeing a ghost. You were the spit'n image of your ma, standing there so straight and proud just the way she used to when we was first married.'

Susan rose, thinking that Paul Kelsey had been a good provider, a steady man who had taken care of her mother and her as long as she could remember. Even if Matt's story was true, Susan could find no fault with her mother or with Paul Kelsey. It was Matt's responsibility to make something out of his life. He could have if he had been man enough. Even if her mother had stayed with him, Susan doubted that he would ever have given them a proper home.

'I'll get up in the morning and cook breakfast for you,' she said.

'No, you get your sleep, honey,' he said. 'I'll be gone, come morning. I just wanted to tell you how it was. You're all I've got to love. A man's in a sorry shape if he don't have nobody to love. That's the way it was with me till I found you.'

She hurried out of the room, afraid even to

look back at him. She had never thought he loved her, never thought that he loved anyone but himself. Now she had heard him say it; she had every reason to think he meant it, and she felt her resolve crumbling. If she stayed in the room talking to him, she would weaken and tell him he could stay.

After she was in bed on the narrow cot in the storeroom, she found she couldn't sleep. She was just too tired, she told herself, too worn out by the excitement of the evening: Glen coming, his fight with Joe Tucker, the bridge being washed out, all that money in the house, the presence of the men who might be the Britton boys. It was enough to wear anyone out, she told herself, then she knew that wasn't the reason she couldn't sleep. The reason was Matt Girard.

If she sent him on in the morning and he was shot or hanged because he was riding a stolen horse, she would never forgive herself. But she couldn't let him stay, either. She would not permit her marriage to be saddled with a man who, by his own admission, had done only one decent thing in his life.

He's got to go, she told herself over and over. She dropped off to sleep with that refrain running through her mind.

# CHAPTER THIRTEEN

Sam Kerwin had reason to know that there was no fool like an old fool. If a man had ever proved it over and over to himself, he had. He'd been proving it for almost a year now. Ever since he'd married Lucy.

Now, walking restlessly around his room and listening to the rain pound on the roof, he asked himself why he had married her. No, that was the wrong question. He knew the answer to that one. He was so much in love with her that he didn't know up from down.

When he thought about it, he wasn't sure that love was the right word. All he knew was that after being married for eleven months, the mere sight of her behind as she walked across the room was enough to set him on fire.

He wasn't old, barely forty, so he guessed it was wrong to call himself old, but he was a fool, all right. A fool over Lucy. After spending a night with her in bed, he felt old. Maybe calling himself an old fool was about right.

But any way he looked at it, the question wasn't why he had married. His first wife had died two years ago and he'd needed a woman. Any rancher needed a woman. As far as that was concerned, any man needed a woman. So, when he met Lucy at a dance in Gold City, he knew as soon as he touched her that she was for him if she'd have him.

He courted her for quite a while before he asked her to marry him. She was only seventeen and he had a terrifying feeling she'd laugh in his face and ask him if he thought she needed a second father. But she didn't. When he got up nerve enough to propose, she said in a matter-of-fact tone, 'Of course I'll marry you. You were so slow I thought I was going to have to pop the question myself.'

At the time he was about the happiest man on Colorado's western slope. He didn't realize until their wedding night that she was the hottest thing since the Chicago fire. It took him a little longer to realize that she had no more morals than a goat, and that she'd crawl into bed with any cowhand who gave her half a chance.

The strange part of it was that it didn't make any difference to the way he felt about her. So far he'd kept a tight rein on her. In the process he'd killed one man and beaten hell out of another one. When he got back home, he'd probably have to kill young Jack West, the only cowhand who worked regularly for him. Kerwin had known when he'd left that it was wrong to leave Lucy alone with Jack, but he'd had no choice. He

112

had to raise some money or he'd lose her, and losing her would be a little worse than dying.

He sat down on the bed and rolled and smoked a cigarette. He tried to consider his problem in a rational manner, but he couldn't. There was simply nothing rational in the way he felt about Lucy. When he'd married her, he had a chunk of money in the bank, a fair-sized herd, and a small ranch on the upper Sundown above Gold City that was clear. He was fairly well off as ranchers went in this country, and now look at him.

Yes, by God, just look at him. First he'd spent all his cash on a wild honeymoon in Denver. Through the months after that she'd wanted this and she'd wanted that, and he'd wound up selling off some of his cattle and mortgaging his spread to Bill Buckner in Gold City to buy her the geegaws she wanted.

Twenty years of hard work gone down a gopher hole. He'd tried a dozen times to call a halt. He'd sworn to himself he wouldn't spend another nickel on her and he'd honestly attempted to explain to her how it was, but she'd crawl up on his lap and run her hands over him and kiss him and he'd wind up promising her the pot of gold at the end of the rainbow, then damned if he wouldn't go out and bust a gut trying to fetch it in for her.

No, the question that rubbed his mind raw wasn't why he had married her. Here he was, Sam Kerwin, forty years old, moderately intelligent, hard-working, honest, steady, looked up to and respected by his neighbors on the upper Sundown, a moral, civic-minded man who served as chairman of the school board even though he had no children. So there was the question. Why would a man like that go on doing the damned fool things he did for Lucy?

He didn't know, but it seemed to him he had become two men, the old Sam Kerwin who kept trying to make him quit being a fool, and the new crazy Sam Kerwin who would do anything Lucy asked him to. The new one always won. That was what made the old Sam so sore about it. He was helpless.

When Lucy told him a week ago she just couldn't stay up there in that wilderness on the Sundown any longer, that he had to take her to Denver, or Grand Junction at least, somewhere else where she could see people and do things, he'd promised her he'd sell the ranch and he'd take her anywhere she wanted to go. She'd kissed him and rewarded him handsomely and he'd ridden off, feeling ten feet tall.

Well, he hadn't sold the ranch. He'd tried his best in Gold City, then started to ride to Cerro, but his horse had gone lame and he'd had to take the stage. He couldn't sell his outfit in Cerro, either. When he went back and told Lucy he'd failed and they'd just have to stay there, she'd pack her suitcase and out she'd go. If she did, he'd shoot himself. He might just as well because he sure didn't want to live without her.

This was the new, crazy Sam Kerwin, of course, the Sam Kerwin who was going to steal the fifty thousand dollars that was downstairs in the dining room in the strongbox. There was nothing the old sane Sam could do to change his mind.

He'd started thinking about it when Moore and Kline had brought the box in from the coach and announced that it held fifty thousand dollars. That was a lot of money even for Lucy to spend. He'd come up to his room as soon as he'd finished eating and started planning what he'd do.

The rain was going to be his lifesaver. His tracks would be washed out before morning. He'd wait until the house was quiet, then he'd go down and offer to spell Moore off. Because he still had the reputation that the old, sane, moral Sam Kerwin had spent years making, Moore would probably accept. If he didn't, Kerwin would knock him out. Or kill him, if he had to. He'd take the box and go out to the barn and saddle a horse and be gone before Logan and Kline knew what was happening.

He wouldn't worry about crossing the Sundown where the bridge had gone out. He'd strike up the river. He knew the rough country where the Sundown headed as well as he knew his own range. Somewhere above his ranch he'd find a place to cross the swollen stream, and then all he'd have to do was to let Lucy see the gold and she'd go with him to China if he said to.

The sane Sam Kerwin tried to argue with him, saying that Glen Logan and Bronc Kline were a couple of tough birds who'd probably shoot him before he got away. Or if they didn't, they'd stay on his trail till hell froze up tight. What was more, it was a long ways to the border, south to the state line and then the full length of New Mexico. He'd never make it with Lucy hanging back and saying she was tired and had to rest. But the new, crazy Sam Kerwin wouldn't listen. All he could think of was that Lucy had to have money, and there it was, at the foot of the stairs just waiting to be taken.

He finished his cigarette and walked to the window. The rain hadn't slacked up a bit. Another hour and he'd be on his way. The house had quieted down. The last sound he'd heard was Susan bringing a couple of men upstairs to a room and then going back down. Apparently everybody was asleep. He opened the door and stood listening. He couldn't hear anything except the steady beat of the rain.

He stepped outside and closed his door. The sooner he got at this the better. He went along the hall and down the stairs, moving silently. He found Reno Moore sitting beside the box, his rifle across his lap, his head tipped forward.

Kerwin could have drawn his gun and slugged him without any trouble, but he hesitated, not sure for a moment whether Moore was asleep or not. Then when he decided to do it and dropped his hand to the butt of his gun, it was too late. Moore stirred and yawned, and then, apparently aware of someone's presence, he looked around and saw Kerwin.

Surprised, Moore asked, 'What the hell are you doing up this time of night, Sam?'

Kerwin had dropped the hand on past his gun butt to his side as soon as Moore stirred. He was sure the guard didn't suspect anything. He said, 'I couldn't sleep with the rain hammering away like it is. I thought I'd come down and take a turn guarding the gold and you could sleep.'

'Now that's right thoughtful,' Moore said, 'but Bronc's coming down pretty soon. I'll wait for him.'

That irritated Kerwin. He didn't want to hurt Moore, but he had a sudden, terrifying feeling that time had run out, that he had already waited too long. He was going to need all the darkness he could get to put miles between him and Logan and Kline when they started after him.

'When's Bronc coming down?' Kerwin asked.

'About midnight, if he wakes up.'

'That's a while yet,' Kerwin said, 'and you were asleep when I showed up. I'm probably not as good a shot as you are, and maybe I don't have the sand in my craw you do, but I'd be a better guard awake than you'd be asleep.'

Moore laughed. 'I guess you might be at that.' He got up and stretched. 'By God, that's no softer'n the seat on the coach.' He picked up the gunny sack. 'Guess I'll take my goober feathers to bed with me. Nobody's gonna have to sit up guarding them.'

He climbed the stairs, yawning loudly. A moment later Kerwin heard his door close. Another five minutes, Kerwin told himself. Everybody but Moore was asleep. In five minutes he'd be sawing it off, too.

He allowed himself some daydreaming then. From what he'd heard, a little American money went a long ways in Mexico. You could buy a hacienda cheap, and you could hire help for close to nothing. He'd lie in bed with Lucy twenty hours out of the twenty-four. He almost laughed aloud when he thought about it. She was always hungry, Lucy was. She'd make an old man

118

out of him quick.

The five minutes he allowed himself was too long. Before it was up, he heard someone on the stairs. He cocked Moore's rifle and turned in his chair. Two men came into sight and stood staring at him, men he hadn't seen before. They must be the late-comers that Susan had taken to their room not long before he came downstairs. One was a fatherly-looking man with a black spade beard, the other one was young and slender with the eyes of a killer.

Kerwin kept them covered as he asked, 'Who are you?'

The young one said insolently, 'What the hell difference does it make who we are?'

Kerwin had a horrible feeling that the young one could move fast if he had to, so fast that he could get his gun out and put a bullet into Kerwin before he could even pull the trigger of the Winchester. He said, 'I'm spelling Reno Moore off for a while. When anyone starts prowling around this time of night, I've got a right to ask who he is.'

'Sure he has, Ted,' the fatherly-looking man said. 'Come on, let's see if there's any coffee on the back of the stove.' He smiled at Kerwin. 'We couldn't sleep, so we thought we'd come down and see if there was any coffee left from supper.'

They walked past Kerwin into the kitchen, the young one looking back over his shoulder and glowering. Kerwin saw a lamp come to life in the kitchen, then heard the rattle of dishes. He was close to panic then. The young one had killer written all over him. Who were they and what were they doing here? Did they know how much money was in the box? If they did, the chances were they aimed to steal it.

Kerwin glanced at the kitchen door, wondering if he had a chance to get out of the house with the box. For once the old, sane Sam Kerwin took control. He told the new, crazy Sam that it would be suicide. The men in the kitchen would hear him and they'd be on his tail before he could reach the front door. Even if he was lucky and killed both of them, which he knew he couldn't, the shooting would wake everybody up and Glen Logan and Bronc Kline would be after him. He'd be out of the frying pan into the fire.

He sat there, clutching Moore's Winchester while sweat ran down his face and his heart beat with great hammering throbs. Sooner or later the men in the kitchen would go back to bed. There was nothing for him to do but just sit here and wait it out.

# CHAPTER FOURTEEN

Matt Girard couldn't sleep. He couldn't forget Glen Logan's question: 'Did you ever do a decent thing, Matt? For Sue or anybody?' Or his answer: 'No, Glen, reckon I never did.'

Matt couldn't remember ever being ashamed of himself before in his life, at least so much ashamed that he couldn't sleep. Outside of whisky, there was nothing he liked as much as sleeping. Here he was, his belly full of good food, lying on a bed in a clean room, with nothing to do but sleep until Susan woke him before dawn and said it was time to move. Still, he couldn't sleep.

In a few hours he'd be riding out, broke, with nothing to do and nowhere to go, and the law looking for him and the stolen horse he was riding. Not that there was anything unusual in the situation. He was familiar with it, but he'd never see Susan again. That bothered him.

Funny how Glen's question hurt. 'Did you ever do a decent thing in your life, Matt?' It had never hurt before. He'd never even thought very much about it. Fifty years of wasted living: getting drunk and lying in the gutter in his own vomit, mooching off everybody and anybody that he could, stealing if he thought it was safe and then spending a big part of his life in jail because of his petty thefts.

No, none of this had ever hurt before. Not the slightest prick of conscience that had been all but dead for many years. But it hurt now because he had found a daughter who had been lost from the time she was a baby, and now he was losing her again because he was plain, damned no good.

After Glen had asked the question, he'd tried to think of least one decent thing he'd done so he could tell Susan. Chances were Glen had told her he'd asked Matt the question and he'd probably told her Matt's answer. The hell of it was that everybody saw him the same way and said the same things about him. No good. Just plain no good. A clod lying in the road that people could step on or walk around. It didn't make much difference. Nobody cared.

Joe Tucker. Molly. Glen. Susan. No matter whom he named, they all had the same opinion of him. Even the Britton boys who had been in jail with him in Cerro dismissed him as the town drunk and talked in front of him as if he didn't exist. Well, he'd thought of one decent thing he'd done. He'd gone to work in a mine in Leadville and he'd held the job and he'd sent money back to his family. One decent thing, he told himself, and he'd been rewarded by having his wife run off with Paul Kelsey.

He'd told Susan about it so she'd be sympathetic and think more of him and less of her mother. Maybe she'd fire Joe Tucker and let him stay. That had been in his mind, all right, but he knew that it had been a vain hope. Firing Joe Tucker or keeping Joe Tucker had nothing to do with it. Susan wanted to marry Glen Logan and right there was the nub of the whole thing.

Now, for the first time in many years, Matt Girard was honest with himself. He could not in any way blame Susan for her attitude towards him. He guessed he couldn't even blame his wife for running away with Paul Kelsey. It was easy enough to say she'd never got a divorce and she'd lived with Kelsey in sin all this time, but when it came to talking about sin, he guessed he was about the biggest sinner there was. Marrying Susan's mother and making her pregnant and then not providing for her and the baby was the biggest sin of all.

He hadn't sent much money from Leadville. That was the truth of it. What he hadn't told Susan was that Kelsey's sister had chewed him out something fierce after he'd gone back. She'd said plain out that Susan and her mother would have starved to death if she and Kelsey hadn't sent food over for weeks until Kelsey finally persuaded her to go away with him.

A sound from the kitchen brought him upright in bed. He had supposed everybody was asleep but him. The house had been quiet for some time, but now a man was puttering around in the kitchen. No, it was more than one man. They were talking, their voices low, so low he couldn't make out the words, but there were at least two of them.

For a few minutes he sat there, listening. He was vaguely disturbed for some reason which he couldn't pin down. He had no reason to be nervous because a couple of men, Glen and the stage driver maybe, had come to the kitchen in the middle of the night to get something to eat. But he was nervous, and he finally decided it was because he knew neither of the voices was Glen's. Maybe one of them was Joe Tucker's.

Matt rose and crossed the room to the door. He put a hand on the knob and hesitated, thinking he'd better let well enough alone. Joe Tucker was the kind who would kill him as he'd threatened to do if he found him here. The door might squeak if he opened it even a crack, and Joe or whoever it was would probably decide to see who was spying on them.

For a time caution and his innate cowardice fought with his curiosity. Finally, largely because there was a familiar ring to the voices which haunted him, curiosity won and he opened the door a crack. He closed it immediately, so quickly that it made a faint sound which he thought they must hear. He stood leaning against the door, his breath coming in heaving pants. Jake and Bud Britton were sitting at the table.

Matt walked back to the bed and sat down, his knees rubbery. He wiped the sweat from his face and tried to think what he should do. He had been truthful in telling Glen he thought the Britton brothers had headed east from Cerro. Neither of them had said a word about coming this way, but now he remembered that Glen had said there was fifty thousand dollars in the house. The money must have been what had brought the outlaws here. He had to think that was it because there was something else that could have made them come this way, something he didn't dare think about and something he knew now he should have told Glen.

He waited impatiently until he didn't hear the hum of voices any longer, the minutes that dragged by the slowest minutes he'd ever experienced in his life. Then, hearing no sound except the beat of the rain or a groaning squeak as a gust of wind struck the house, he slipped back to the door, opening it a fraction of an inch, and stared through the crack. The outlaws were gone, and the lamp had been blown out. The only light came from the dining room.

He slipped out of the bedroom and crossed the kitchen to the storeroom where Susan was sleeping. He kept watching the dining room door. Someone was still up or the lamp wouldn't be burning in there. He had no idea who it was. The Brittons maybe. Or Joe Tucker.

He didn't dare let either the Brittons or Tucker know he was here, so he had to wake Susan. She'd be safe if it was Tucker or Glen or the stage driver. If it was either of the Brittons ... No, it couldn't be. He refused even to consider the possibility.

He opened the storeroom door and stepped into the room. In the thin light he located the cot. He crossed to it, breathing hard because he was as scared as he had ever been in his life. He was being a coward again, for if the Brittons were in the dining room, he was sending Susan to her death just as he'd be sending himself if he went. Then he remembered that he didn't know which room Glen was in, so he told himself it had to be Susan.

He knelt beside the bed and shook Susan awake. She sat up and would have screamed if he hadn't clapped a big hand over her mouth. 'It's me, Susie. Your pa. You've got to do something for me.' Startled out of a deep sleep, she started to struggle, then what he said got through to her and she sat motionless, waiting for him to take his hand away from her mouth.

When he withdrew his hand, she said angrily, 'I just got to sleep...'

'It's important,' he whispered. 'I guess it's about the most important thing that either one of us ever did. You've got to go upstairs and wake Glen and have him come down here. I've got to tell him something.'

'You've had plenty of chance to tell him anything you had to,' she said, her anger growing. 'I don't see any reason for you to wake me up...'

'I wouldn't have done it,' he broke in, 'if it wasn't a matter of us living or dying. I've got to see Glen.'

'Why?'

He hesitated, not wanting to tell her. Finally he said, 'The Britton boys were sitting at the table drinking coffee a while ago. I've got to tell Glen.'

She was silent a moment as if thinking over what he'd said, then she rose and slipped into a robe. 'All right, I'll get him.'

He asked, 'Who's in the dining room?'

'Reno Moore, I guess. He was guarding the strongbox when I came to bed.'

He returned to his room and shut the door and sat down on the edge of the bed. he began to shake. He tried to tell himself that this was a decent thing he was doing. Even Glen would admit that. It wasn't easy for a coward to do a brave thing, and he was being brave. If the Brittons saw him, they'd shoot him on sight. Chances were he was the only man in the house who could identify them, and they wouldn't want to be identified until they made their move.

Glen came in a moment later, cranky and thoroughly disgusted at being roused from a sleep he needed. Shutting the door, he said, 'I figured I'd get about three or four hours sleep before I had to get up to guard that damned money, but no, you couldn't even let me have that much. I kept asking you if you knew anything and you kept saying you didn't ...'

'I didn't,' Matt broke in, his voice shaky. 'I told you I thought the Britton brothers were going east, and I did think so. They kept saying that before the rest of us, but they lied or changed their plan. They're in this house right now.'

'I figured that's who they were,' Glen said. 'That what you woke me up for?'

'If you thought it was them,' Matt demanded, 'why didn't you have me identify 'em before now?'

'In the first place you might have been in the game with them to steal the fifty thousand dollars,' Glen said bluntly. 'In the second place, I never know when I can believe you and when I can't. You're the biggest liar I ever saw. Sometimes I think you'd rather lie than tell the truth. If you're insulted, start thinking about the lies you've told me and then shut up.'

Matt looked at him and then at the floor. Glen was right. He hadn't done anything to earn the right to be believed, but Glen had to believe him now. He looked up and said, 'I'm telling you the truth now, Glen. I'd have told you before but I figured all they was thinking about was beating the rope. I guess I was wrong. I had the cell next to 'em in Cerro. I slept most of the time, so they didn't pay no attention to me. They talked like I wasn't there. Of course they didn't know I was Susie's pa.'

He stopped and swallowed, and Glen said impatiently, 'All right, what are you trying to say?'

'Well, I'm thinking maybe they're here to kill Susie. I dunno if they've heard about the dinero or not, but they're the ones who murdered Susie's ma and Paul Kelsey. I heard 'em talking about it. Bud, he's the mean one, kept saying they should have killed her before, but Jake, he said no, that she wouldn't know 'em now if she seen 'em again. Bud kept arguing about it. Said she'd be a witness against 'em someday and they oughtta come back and rub her out. Well, when I seen 'em just now, I figured maybe that was what they were here for.'

Glen's dark face had turned white. He stared at Matt, loathing. He said, 'You

God-damned idiot! If you'd told me that in the first place, we'd have taken them on suspicion when they first showed up. Now we have to take them the best way we can, and maybe get shot doing it.'

He wheeled and stalked out, leaving the door open. Matt rose and shut the door, then sprawled out on the bed, shaking uncontrollably. If the Brittons ever found out that he had told Glen what he'd heard in the Cerro jail, they'd kill him just as surely as the sun would come up in the morning.

## CHAPTER FIFTEEN

Sam Kerwin felt as if he had taken a seat at a busy street corner. First the two strangers walked past him into the kitchen and had their coffee. Presently they came back, ignoring him this time. He covered them with the cocked Winchester from the moment they entered the dining room until they reached the foot of the stairs and climbed to the hall above. They pretended they didn't know they were under the rifle. Even the young one, who had been insolent and contemptuous before as they'd walked past, now acted as if Kerwin simply wasn't there.

He relaxed after the two men were out of

sight, the old, sane Sam Kerwin arguing that he'd better forget this whole crazy business and sit tight until Bronc Kline came down to relieve him. The new Sam Kerwin would have no part of it. He couldn't think of anything except Lucy's face when he told her he'd brought her fifty thousand dollars; he'd tell her they were lighting out for Mexico where they'd buy a hacienda and hire a passel of servants and he'd dress her like a queen. Then he'd show her the money, and that night after they were in bed...

Suddenly he became aware that the house was absolutely quiet. It was time to move. Someone else might come by. Or the rain would stop. He wanted to leave while it was still coming down hard so they wouldn't be able to track him.

He rose, paused to listen again, and stooped to lift the box just as Susan Girard entered the room from the kitchen. She was barefooted, so she hadn't made the slightest sound. Not having heard her in the kitchen, he had no idea she was out of bed until she hurried past him.

Quickly he straightened and put a hand on the small of his back as if he had merely stood up to stretch. He knew he looked as guilty as hell, but he didn't say anything and she didn't, either.

Her eyes were wide open. She stared straight ahead, not looking once to either side. After she turned up the stairs, the thought occurred to him that she wasn't seeing anything. Maybe she was sleepwalking. He might just as well pick up the box and be on his way. She wouldn't know if he was there or not if she did come back.

He stooped again. This time he had the box a foot off the floor when he heard Susan talking to someone upstairs. He remained motionless, bent over that way with the heavy box in his hands, listening, then he heard them on the stairs. He eased the box back down and was just straightening up when Susan and Glen Logan rushed past him toward the kitchen.

Neither said a word or even appeared to notice him. Susan still had that strange, tight expression on her face as if she weren't aware of anything around her. Logan had pulled his pants over his underclothes and was in his sock feet.

This was crazy, Kerwin told himself. He wondered if he had suddenly become invisible. He stood there, staring at the kitchen door as he considered this sudden rush of activity. Something was going on. He was sure of that. Belatedly it occurred to him that Logan had a different expression on his face than the girl had on hers. He just looked grumpy and sour-tempered as any man would who had been roused from a deep sleep.

Kerwin heard a door close in the kitchen, then a second one. Apparently they had gone into different rooms. For several minutes he stood listening, wondering why Logan had come downstairs and whether he would go back up to his room. Of all the men in the house, Kerwin had the greatest respect for Logan. He knew his reputation in Gold City. Good with his fists, fast with a gun, and all the guts in the world.

If anyone else except Logan had gone by, Kerwin told himself, he would have been on his way. But Logan might come out of the kitchen just as Kerwin was crossing the dining room with the strongbox in his hands. Logan would shoot and then ask what he was doing with the money. No, not even the new crazy Sam Kerwin would take a chance with Glen Logan.

For a little while, then, the old, sane Sam Kerwin was in charge. He was standing beside the box, the Winchester in his hands, when Logan strode out of the kitchen, his face as expressionless as Susan's had been a few minutes before.

When Logan reached him, Kerwin said, 'What's going on?'

Logan kept on as if he didn't hear. Apparently the question got through to him just as he reached the foot of the stairs. He stopped and swung around, questioning eyes on Kerwin. He asked, 'You guarding the money?'

Kerwin nodded. 'I took Moore's place. He said Kline would come and spell me off after a while, and then you'd take the job till daylight.'

Logan chewed on his lower lip, eyes still probing Kerwin as if not quite sure of his appraisal of the man. Finally he asked, 'Are you pretty good with that Winchester?'

'Fair,' Kerwin said.

'You may get a chance to use it,' Logan said. 'I just found out those two strangers who rode in late this evening are the Britton brothers. I thought that's who they were, but I wasn't sure. Now I am. I'm getting Kline up and we're going to take them. If they get past us, it'll be up to you. Watch the stairs. Let 'em have it in the belly. Don't get soft-hearted because they've got two legs and walk like men. They aren't. They're murdering sons of bitches. Both of them.'

Logan went on up the stairs. For a moment the old, sane Sam Kerwin still held the controls. He argued that the only thing to do was to sit tight. Let Logan and Kline handle the outlaws. Stay right here and guard the money.

Then the moment was gone. He thought of Lucy and he thought of the fifty thousand dollars, and he knew he wasn't man enough to handle the Brittons if they did get past

Logan and Kline. They'd blow his head off on general principles. He'd heard enough about young Bud Britton to know that was the way he operated. If he was ever going to make a try for that money, he had to do it now.

He picked up the box, shifted it so he held it under one arm, then grabbed up the Winchester and headed across the dining room toward the hall door, his heart so high in his throat he couldn't swallow. If he could make it into the hall...

He didn't. From the stairs Jake Britton yelled, 'Drop that box.'

Kerwin's heart plummeted like a dropped stone. He took one more headlong step, but he was still two more steps from the hall door when he heard the roar of a gun and saw splinters flying from the door casing ahead of him.

He let the box crash to the floor. He whirled, bringing the Winchester up and easing back the hammer, but he never got off the shot. Both Brittons were rushing down the stairs. Jake Britton had fired the first warning shot. His gun was still smoking. Now the young one squeezed the trigger of his gun just as his boots hit the floor at the foot of the stairs.

This was not a warning shot. The bullet slammed into Kerwin's chest and knocked him down. As he fell, he tried to call out to

135

Lucy. It seemed to him he was falling headlong down a dark tunnel. For one brief, splendid moment he saw Lucy's face at the far end of the tunnel, then it was gone and there was nothing but blackness, and then there was nothing.

## CHAPTER SIXTEEN

Glen was shaking Bronc Kline awake when he heard the Britton boys run along the hall, and he knew at once he had made a mistake. Sam Kerwin wouldn't stop them. Glen should have kept them bottled in their room. If he had stayed in the hall—No, it wouldn't have made any difference. His gun was still in his room. They'd have cut him like a big, fat turkey.

Kline's revolver was in his holster on the floor at the head of the bed. Glen yanked it free from leather. As he whirled toward the door, he heard the Britton boys' boots clatter on the stairs, he heard Jake yell at Kerwin, and as he ran out of the room, he heard the shots.

Bronc Kline sat up in bed, demanding, 'What's going on?'

Glen didn't stop to explain. He was halfway down the stairs when Jake Britton called, 'Drop your gun, Logan.' Britton fired once, the bullet snapping past Glen's right ear. He stopped, knowing the next wouldn't go on past. He was far enough down the stairs so that he could see across the dining room to the hall door. Britton was standing beside Kerwin's body. Bud wasn't in sight. The box was gone.

Kline and Moore crowded against Glen. Neither was armed. Both had jumped out of bed when they'd heard the shots and had run into the hall without taking time even to pull on their pants. Glen hesitated a second, frozen there halfway down the stairs. The gun was in his right hand at his side. If he lifted it, if he moved it in any way, he'd be dead. He was lucky it was Jake and not Bud standing there with his gun on him or he'd be dead now. Reluctantly he let the gun drop and heard it thump on the stairs as it slid almost to the dining room floor before it stopped on one of the steps. Moore and Kline started to curse, then were silent when Britton snapped, 'Shut up.'

Britton moved forward so he could see the top of the stairs. 'Who else is up there?'

'A preacher named Harlan Wells,' Glen answered, 'and a woman named Mrs. Avery and her boy Frosty.'

'That's all?'

'That's all.'

The outlaw motioned toward the kitchen door. 'Who's back there?'

'Susan Girard,' Glen said. 'She owns the place. She's the one who waited on you tonight.'

'I know who she is,' Britton said impatiently. 'Who else?'

'Her help, Joe Tucker and his wife Molly.'

'That all?'

Glen had thought of the possibility that Matt Girard would hear the shooting and then blunder out of his room. If he did, the sight of him might be enough to set Britton off on a shooting spree. But Matt was a coward and he could probably stay where it was safe. In any case it was a chance Glen had to take. He said, 'That's all.'

Britton laughed, a tight nervous sound. 'Well then, I guess I've got all the tough hands right where I want 'em. Now you stand pat. Bud's saddling our horses and we'll be traveling pronto. If any of you come busting out through the front door, you'll get it.' He dug a toe into Kerwin's ribs. 'You'll be dead meat just like this bucko.'

'What'd you kill Sam for?' Glen demanded.

'Why, he was a damned thief,' Britton said indignantly. 'He was stealing the money. We couldn't stand for that after all the trouble we'd taken to get here.'

'You mean you knew the stage was carrying a load of gold?' Glen asked.

'We sure did,' Britton said. 'We had a tip

138

she was loaded. We rode east from town, circled and stopped at the Vance place where I got that wallet I showed you, then we came here. Just one thing went wrong. We didn't expect the bridge to be out. Now we've got to head upstream and hide out in the hills for a while until the heat's off and we can get to Mexico.'

'Who gave you the tip?' Glen asked.

'You're gabbing too much,' Britton said. 'Shut up.'

That was all the talk. Britton was a planner; he had said what he aimed to say and that was all he was going to say. What he had said had been for a purpose, but at the moment Glen couldn't figure out what it was. He stood there, Kline and Moore motionless behind him, thinking he had never felt quite as helpless in his life as he did at this moment. There was nothing he could do until Bud Britton brought the horses and Jake left the house. To be alive then was the best he could hope for.

One fear sent a chill down Glen's back. Jake might tell him or one of the men behind him to get Susan, then he would shoot her down in cold blood. But if he did, he'd have to kill the rest of them, too, because they'd all be witnesses. No, it wasn't likely to happen, Glen told himself, and again he was thankful that it was Jake, not Bud, who was holding them on the stairs.

Glen had no idea of time, but it seemed to him that young Britton was taking an eternity to saddle the horses. The only one who spoke was Reno Moore who whispered, 'Why'n hell did I ever let Sam spell me off? I got him killed for it.'

Glen didn't say anything. He didn't feel like talking. He sensed from the tension that gripped Jake Britton that it wouldn't take much to set him off, perhaps no more than a wrong word. So they waited in silence, the minutes dragging out, then they heard Bud call from in front of the house.

'Stay right where you are,' Britton said. 'You come after us and you'll get a dose of hot lead.'

He backed through the doorway and disappeared into the hall. Kline put a foot on the step below him. Glen whispered, 'Wait.'

Jake Britton popped back into view, grinning. 'Good. You listen fine. Three little Injuns on the stairs. One came down for a gun and then there was only two.'

He disappeared into the hall again. Kline muttered, 'The sneaking bastard! He was looking for an excuse to kill us.'

'Maybe,' Glen said, 'but he's a smart booger. Maybe he just aimed to scare us into standing here.'

He thought he heard the front door open, thought he caught a flicker of light in the hall as if a gust of wind had struck the bracket lamp. Whether this was another trick or not, he knew he could not stand here another second.

He lunged down the stairs, stooping to scoop up the gun, and raced across the dining room. He heard Kline yell, 'Don't be a fool, Glen.' And Moore, 'All they got was some rocks.'

But he didn't stop. He rushed to the front door and yanked it open and plunged through it onto the porch, moving fast and at an angle so he wouldn't be silhouetted against the light for more than a second. It was long enough to draw a bullet from the darkness. He fired until the gun was empty, aiming first at the powder flash and then spreading his shots.

He heard the sound of hoofs in the mud. He stood on the porch, listening. They were out there in the darkness and the rain, but only by the wildest stretch of luck could he have hit one of them. Then he understood why Jake Britton had made all that talk about circling the town and seeing the Vances and coming here. He'd carefully said, 'We've got to head upstream and hide in the hills.' But they weren't going upstream. They were going down the river, so obviously they had no intention of hiding in the hills.

They'd go as far as they could tonight in the storm, hoping that if there was any
141

pursuit, it would be in the opposite direction. Somewhere they'd find a place to cross the swollen river and they'd line out for Mexico. But there was a strong possibility that they'd stop to look at the gold and discover that the box was full of rocks. If they did that, they'd be back, and this time maybe Bud would be facing them with a gun, not Jake.

When Glen returned to the dining room, he saw that Joe Tucker stood by the table buttoning his shirt, his eyes on Kerwin's body. He lifted his head, his tiny red eyes on Glen.

'You got a dead man on your hands, Logan,' Tucker said. 'What was all the shooting about?'

Glen didn't answer. He looked at Moore and Kline who were standing uncertainly at the foot of the stairs as if not sure what they should do now. Glen asked, 'How do you suppose Sam got over here?'

'Maybe he was trying to steal the box,' Moore said.

Glen shook his head. 'I don't think so. I've known Sam quite a while and he never struck me as a thief.'

'You never knew him to have a chance at fifty thousand dollars before, either,' Moore said. 'Well, I'm going back to bed. They're gone and we can't do anything for Kerwin.'

'Gone?' Tucker shouted. 'Now just a damn minute. I asked what was going on around here.'

'It took you a long time to get your clothes on,' Glen said. 'You've got a gun. If you'd showed up in time, you could have plugged Jake. Chances are Bud would have come in to help his brother and we'd have got him, but no, you just snuggled closer to Molly till the shooting was over.'

Tucker's face turned red. 'Jake,' he said. 'Bud. Are you talking about the Britton boys?'

'That's exactly who I'm talking about,' Glen said. 'They took off with the money the stage was carrying.'

Tucker stared at him, his face going white, his little eyes bulging from his head so it seemed they were about to pop out of their sockets. For a time his breath sawed in and out of his big chest, then he said, 'You mean they rode clean away?'

'That's what they did,' Glen said.

Tucker began to curse as if he had gone crazy. He threw out a big hand toward Moore and Kline. 'Get dressed. Get your guns. We're going after them.'

He whirled toward the kitchen and disappeared through the door. Glen, glancing at Moore and Kline, sensed that the same question was in their minds that was in his. After carefully staying out of the trouble, why should Joe Tucker get so excited now about going after the Brittons?

# CHAPTER SEVENTEEN

Glen returned Kline's gun as they went up the stairs. Neither said anything until they had dressed and Glen had buckled his own gun around his waist and had stepped back into the hall. Moore joined him, asking, 'You going after them?'

Glen shook his head. A moment later Kline came out of his room. Glen said in a low voice, 'You've been on this run quite a while, Bronc. I guess you know Tucker better'n I do. How do you figure him?'

'I've never figured him out,' Kline said. 'He's been working for Susan for a long time. Before that he worked for Paul Kelsey. He's a surly bastard, but he's a good hand with horses. He could make twice as much in Gold City as here. Don't ask me why he's stayed. I've often wondered, but I sure don't know.'

Glen turned to Moore. 'What do you think, Reno?'

'I don't think at all,' Moore answered. 'I never liked Tucker, so I ain't had much to do with him. Besides, I ain't been riding shotgun as long as Bronc's been driving this run, but it strikes me that Tucker might be in cahoots with the Brittons.'

'I've been thinking the same,' Glen said,

'but it seems about as reasonable as saying Sam Kerwin was trying to steal the gold.'

From the foot of the stairs Tucker called, 'We're wasting time. Let's ride.'

'We'd better play this out a little,' Glen said. 'Bronc, we'll go out to the barn with him. If we're going to have trouble with him, I'd rather have it out there than here in the house where it will upset Susan.'

Moore went downstairs with Glen and Kline who walked on across the dining room into the hall and put on their hats and slickers. When Tucker, who was wearing his slicker, saw that Moore made no move to get his, he said impatiently, 'Come on, come on. We ought to be on the move now. What the hell's holding you up?'

'I'm not going,' Moore said. 'I don't feel well. My stummick's upset.'

Glen and Kline stepped back into the dining room in time to see Tucker move toward Moore, so furious he was trembling. 'They got the box you was supposed to be guarding, didn't they?' Tucker demanded. 'You're yellow, Moore, just too damned yellow.'

Moore took a quick step forward and swung his right. It started from his knees and Tucker had every chance in the world to block the blow, but he didn't. Glen never knew why unless Tucker was so blinded by his anger that he didn't see the blow coming

145

until it was too late. In any case, Moore caught him squarely on the point of the chin, knocking him flat on his back.

Tucker didn't get up for a moment. He raised himself on an elbow and shook the cobwebs out of his head, then he scrambled to his feet and would have lunged at Moore if Glen and Kline hadn't grabbed his arms and held him.

'That's enough, Tucker,' Glen said. 'You called the wrong man yellow. Go on to bed, Reno.'

Moore wheeled and disappeared up the stairs. Glen and Kline retained their grip on Tucker's arms until he said, 'All right, all right. Let's ride.'

They went out into the rain and slogged through the mud to the barn. Tucker lighted a match, but the lantern which usually hung just inside the door was gone. 'They must have got rid of it,' Tucker said. 'There's another one back here. I'll get it.'

Glen and Kline waited as Tucker strode along the dark runway. Kline whispered, 'How far do you figure to play the string out?'

'To here,' Glen answered. 'No farther.'

A moment later Tucker returned with the lighted lantern. He said, 'Kline, take that bay in the back stall.' He hung the lantern on the nail in the wall and turned to his saddle when he saw that neither Glen nor Kline had moved. He dropped his hand to his side and faced them, red eyes swinging from Glen to Kline and back to Glen.

'What's wrong now?' Tucker demanded. 'You don't look any more anxious to find the Brittons than that yellow-bellied guard.'

'We've got a question to ask,' Glen said. 'I guess this is as good a time to ask it as any. You're packing an iron, aren't you?'

'Sure.' Tucker patted his slicker where it covered the holstered gun. 'You think I'd start after the Brittons with nothing but my fists?'

'You had the gun in your room,' Glen said. 'Why didn't you show up as soon as Jake Britton fired the first shot?'

'I figured it wasn't my fight,' Tucker said.

'I'm not going to be fool enough to call you yellow,' Glen said. 'I know you're not just as well as you knew Reno Moore wasn't, so I figure you had your reasons for laying in bed.'

'If we're guessing about reasons,' Tucker threw back, 'let's guess at yours. If you knew they was the Brittons, why didn't you get 'em when you had a chance?'

'I didn't know for sure who they were,' Glen said. 'I'd never seen them. Neither had Reno or Bronc here. With three women in the house, I didn't want to start any trouble that could be avoided so we decided to wait it out. If they hadn't been the Brittons, there wouldn't have been any trouble.'

'You could have got me out of bed,' Tucker said. 'I could have identified 'em. We'd have had 'em right here without no trouble and they wouldn't have got the money.'

'I didn't know you'd ever seen 'em,' Glen said.

'Yeah,' Tucker said. 'Once.'

'Where?'

'I disremember,' Tucker said sullenly. 'It was quite a while ago. But I'd a knowed 'em, all right. Hell, they've been in the Cerro jail for a spell. We've all heard enough about 'em to recognize 'em. You're both idiots or you were afraid to tangle with 'em. Or maybe you're hooked up with 'em. All I know is that this whole business looks damned fishy to me.'

'Oh hell,' Kline said in disgust. 'Let's go back into the house. You're not gonna find out anything from this huckleberry.'

'Wait,' Glen said. 'Joe, I want to know where and when you saw the Britton boys.'

Tucker was boxed and he knew it. All he could say was, 'I guess I never seen 'em, but I saw their pictures and I'd a knowed 'em, and so should you.'

'Somebody got a gun to them in the Cerro jail,' Glen said, 'And somebody tipped them off about the stage carrying a heavy load of gold. Maybe you fit into the pattern

148

somewhere.'

'Hogwash,' Tucker snapped. 'I'm the one who wants to go after 'em, ain't I? You're the one who's doing the jawing while they get farther away all the time. Maybe you're getting a cut and you know where to find 'em tomorrow sometime.'

'We're not going after them,' Glen said. 'Not unless you know where they'd hole up.'

'How would I know?' Tucker demanded. 'Hell, I just say we've got to go after 'em.'

'In the dark and the rain?' Glen asked. 'Which direction would we go?'

'Why, they'll head ...' Tucker stopped, his small red eyes narrowing as he saw the trap Glen had laid for him and backed away from it. 'How would I know about that, either. I guess they'd head for the state line. They can't cross the river here, so they'll ride downstream until they find a place where they can cross it and then they'll head for New Mexico.'

'Glen, let's go back to the house,' Kline said impatiently. 'It'll be a hell of a note if they sneak into the house while we're out here and we walk in on 'em.'

'Why would they come back?' Tucker demanded.

'Because they didn't get the money,' Glen said. 'The box was a decoy filled with rocks. Moore's got the dinero in his room.'

He watched Tucker's face closely; he saw

149

the pendulous-lipped mouth drop open in surprise, saw an expression of relief cross the big man's face, then it was blotted out by a sudden rush of anger.

'You made a fool out of me, didn't you?' Tucker said bitterly. 'All this talk about chasing 'em was just play-acting, wasn't it? You feel any better, now that you've had your fun?'

Glen drew his revolver. It was in his hand before Tucker could make a move. He said, 'Pull your iron slow and drop it and back up. Someway or another you're into this up to your dirty neck. I'll feel better when you're dead. If you make a wrong move, I'll fix it so you are.'

Tucker obeyed, cursing angrily. After he had backed up along the runway, Glen moved forward and, picking up the gun, handed it to Kline. He said, 'Even if they'd got the money, we wouldn't chase them, Joe. I wouldn't go off and leave Susan. I guess you know they killed her mother and Paul Kelsey. She didn't recognize them, but they may think she did. There's a chance they'll come back to kill her.'

Again Glen watched Tucker's face closely. He saw the man was shocked by surprise. He wasn't sure of anything else.

'Where'd you hear that?' Tucker demanded.

'Where I heard it is my business,' Glen

said. 'I'm wondering if that was when you saw the Brittons.'

'You're a fool,' Tucker said wearily. 'I wasn't here when it happened. Neither was Molly. You've sure been eating loco weed. They had a chance to plug her tonight. They won't come back for that. Besides, it don't make any difference about Kelsey and Susan's ma. The Brittons are gonna swing for beefing that stage driver on the other side of Cerro.'

'Sure,' Glen agreed, 'but a man like Bud Britton doesn't think logically about things like that. If he figures Susan is dangerous to him, he'll kill her. What I'm afraid of is they'll find out they've got rocks instead of gold. If they do, they'll be back. Maybe they'll kill all of us. You should have thought of that before you hooked up with them.'

'Oh, for God's sake,' Tucker said. 'I never got hooked up with 'em. If there's anybody I don't want hurt, it's Susan. You ought to know that.'

'I used to think that,' Glen said. 'Now I'm not sure, but I'll tell you one thing, Joe. I'm marrying her. She'll come to live with me and sell out here, or I'll sell out and move in here. Either way, you're fired.'

'All right,' Tucker said. 'If she marries a bastard like you, I don't want to work for her.'

'Now can we go into the house?' Kline

asked. 'Every minute we stay out here we're taking a chance.'

'Grab the lantern and go ahead,' Glen said. 'It hasn't been a waste of time if that's what you're thinking, Bronc.'

Kline took the lantern off the nail. 'You showed your hole card,' he said sourly, 'but I didn't catch him showing his.'

Glen backed into an empty stall, motioning for Tucker to follow Kline. He didn't say anything. Kline was just about right. Glen's suspicion of Tucker was still only suspicion. He didn't have enough to hold the man for the Cerro sheriff. Not unless he could get something out of Molly and he didn't think he could. She was still Tucker's wife no matter what she knew or believed about him.

They trudged back to the house through the mud, the cold rain driving at them. They cleaned their boots on the scraper and went in, Glen still undecided what he would do with Tucker. Kline took off his slicker and hat and hung them on the hall tree. He said, 'I'm going to look in on Reno.'

Glen nodded as he hung up his slicker and hat. Stepping back, he motioned for Tucker to do the same. Tucker obeyed, then swung around, grinning mockingly. 'You're forgetting one little thing, Logan. If the Britton boys do come back, you'll need every man you've got and that includes me. I'm pretty handy with an iron. Better think that over.'

Glen nodded for him to go into the dining room, thinking that he'd better get Susan up and put Tucker in the storeroom. It was tight with only one small window. The door could be locked from the kitchen side. As far as Glen knew, it was the only room in the house that could be locked.

'Glen,' Kline yelled from the head of the stairs. 'Get up here. Pronto.'

Tucker ran across the dining room and took the stairs three at a time, Glen a step behind him. Kline's voice had held an urgency which was not to be ignored. Glen had a terrifying premonition of what he would find, and yet when he stood in the doorway of Reno Moore's room and stared at his motionless body that lay face down on the floor beside the bed, he found it hard to believe that this was reality. It must be a nightmare, something he had been afraid would happen and so now he was dreaming it.

Tucker was shaking Kline's shoulders. 'The money?' Tucker demanded. 'He had the money?'

'He had it,' Kline said bitterly, 'but he sure don't have it now.' He faced Glen, his face grim. 'You and your God-damned walk through the mud. While we're out there palavering with this son of a bitch, somebody

153

comes in here and knocks Reno out and gets away with the whole cheese. What have you got to say about that, Logan?'

This was no dream. It was horrible reality. Glen looked at Kline, but he didn't say anything. There wasn't anything he could say. He knew exactly what the stage driver was thinking, that he'd schemed this out with someone in the house and he'd furnished the diversion that had made the robbery possible. Kline had no proof against him, but then, Glen had no proof against Joe Tucker, either.

## CHAPTER EIGHTEEN

Glen nodded at Kline. 'Is Reno alive?'

Kline looked surprised. 'Why hell, I don't know. I saw him lying here and he wasn't moving. I just figured he was dead.'

Glen knelt beside Moore and felt his pulse. 'He's all right, I think. It's strong and steady. He just got a good wallop on the head.'

Glen slipped one arm under Moore's neck and the other under his knees and, lifting him from the floor, laid him on the bed. A thin trickle of blood had run down his forehead and had dried there. Glen ran gentle fingers over the man's head, found the knot where he had been struck, and stepped back. He looked at Kline and saw suspicion clearly stamped on his face: he turned to Tucker and saw the smoldering fury in his eyes.

'You aimed to have that money, didn't you, Joe?' Glen asked.

'You're damned right I did,' Tucker said. 'Fifty thousand dollars would have set me up for life.'

'That why you stuck around here all this time?' Glen asked. 'You figured that sooner or later a windfall like this would drop into your lap?'

'That's as good a reason as any,' Tucker said bitterly.

Glen turned to Kline who had not put his suspicion into words. He said, 'I don't know any more about where the money is than you do, Bronc, but right now I guess we're all interested in the same thing. That's finding it. Now it looks to me like it's got to be in the house. If the Brittons had come back, we'd have heard them. They'd have got somebody out of the bed and tried to make them tell where the money was. That reasonable?'

Tucker nodded. 'They'd have started with Susan. As much as I want that dinero, I couldn't hold out if I seen 'em start carving on her.'

Kline grunted, an incoherent sound that meant nothing. Glen turned on him

155

savagely. 'Say what you've got in your head, Bronc. You think I took you and Joe out to the barn so somebody could come up here and knock Reno and take the money. Well, I didn't. I guess fifty thousand dollars is enough to make any of us go crooked, so it might have been you. Maybe Sam Kerwin really was trying to steal it when the Brittons shot him. Maybe Reno hid it and knocked himself out. How about it?'

Kline grinned, suddenly abashed. 'All right, Glen, I guess we start with the notion that you'n me and Reno didn't do it. If Tucker hadn't been with us, I'd say he was our man.'

'We can discount the women, I think,' Glen said. 'The kid, too. Near as I can tell, Reno was hit just once. It had to be a hell of a wallop. Molly's the only one strong enough to do it.'

Glen studied Tucker, wondering if it had been Molly and Tucker knew it. No, not good-natured, hard-working Molly who thought of Susan as her own daughter. He'd be blaming Susan next. He said, 'Harlan Wells is the only man up here. I sure can't think it was him.'

'He's the only one left,' Kline said, 'if you don't consider the women, but I ain't sure you can throw the women out so easy. Molly's Tucker's wife. I doubt that she's any better'n he is in the pinch. Mrs. Avery wouldn't have to teach school if she had it. With the kid's help, I guess they could have handled Reno. And even if you think Susan is . . .'

'Don't say it,' Tucker broke in. 'Don't say it. Lay it on Molly if you want to. Go down there and search our room. It could of been the Avery woman and her kid. I didn't see 'em, but Molly told me about 'em. Just don't say anything about Susan. If her old man was here. . .'

'Matt,' Glen said softly. 'Why, he is here. I completely forgot about him.'

Glen rushed past Tucker into the hall and down the stairs, Tucker right behind him shouting, 'Is that old bastard in the house?'

'He's here,' Glen said, and picking up the lamp from the dining room table, ran into the kitchen.

'I told him I'd twist his neck if he ever came back,' Tucker said. 'So help me, I'll . . .'

'No you won't,' Glen said. 'We don't want him dead. We want to know where the money is.'

He opened the door of Susan's bedroom and went in. Matt lay on top of the covers, his clothes on, snoring loudly. Glen set the lamp on the bureau and turned in time to see Tucker grab Matt's feet and pull him off the bed. He hit the floor with a jarring thump. He let out a yelp of pain and sat up, then he saw Tucker's face ugly with temper and dropped back to the floor, groaning.

'Where is it?' Tucker shouted. 'Where the hell is it?'

Glen shoved Tucker back. 'I'll talk to him. Here, sit on the bed, Matt. You've got a little talking to do, so you'd better get comfortable.' Matt pulled himself up. He sat on the edge of the bed, his frightened eyes on Glen, then swung his gaze to Tucker and back to Glen. 'Now then,' Glen said, 'where's the money?'

Bewildered, Matt said, 'I don't have no money. I'm broke. I told you that, Glen. I got out of the Cerro jail and I stole a horse and I came here. I didn't get no chance to get any money.'

'The money the stage was carrying,' Glen said. 'The fifty thousand dollars I told you was in the house. Where did you put it?'

Matt stared at Glen as if he thought Glen was out of his mind. 'I didn't put it nowhere. I couldn't. I never had it. I don't know nothing about it.'

'Oh hell, Logan,' Tucker said. 'Let me do it. I'll have it out of him in about a minute or I'll beat him into a hunk of raw meat.'

'No,' Glen said. 'He's going to have a chance to talk. Let's go into the kitchen, Matt. Maybe you'd like a cup of coffee. I'll build the fire up if you do. Fetch the lamp, Joe.'

Kline had been standing in the doorway. He said, 'I'd go easy on the old boy, Glen. He seemed mighty surprised. I don't think he's that good an actor.'

'He's a good liar,' Glen said. 'He's the best liar I've ever seen. You never believe the first thing he tells you.'

Glen jerked his head at the door. Matt rose and rubbed his tail bone. 'You had no cause to jerk me off the bed,' he said to Tucker. 'That hurt.'

Tucker was holding the lamp. He grinned as he looked at the flame and then at Matt. 'You'll hurt some more if you don't tell us what you done with that money. Ever have your fingers held over a burning lamp, old man? One at a time, and then start over, all ten fingers?'

Matt recoiled in horror. 'That sounds like an Apache trick. You wouldn't do anything like that.'

'I wouldn't?' Tucker laughed. 'Old man, I'm the one who taught the Apaches everything they know. I told you to stay away from here and you're sure going to wish you had. You'll wish you'd left that money alone, too, if you don't tell us what you done with it.'

'Come on,' Glen said. 'Out here.'

Matt tottered out of the bedroom and across the kitchen and collapsed into a chair at the table. He said, 'I didn't think you'd

159

ever do anything like this, Glen. I don't have the money. I never stole nothing big in my life. If the money's gone, the Brittons must have taken it. Or Tucker here. He's mighty anxious to lay it onto me.'

Tucker moved toward him, his big hands fisted. Glen shoved him back. 'Not yet, Joe. Now then, Matt, it's like this. The Brittons shot and killed Sam Kerwin who was guarding the box that they figured had the money in it. They lit out on their horses, but the box didn't have anything but rocks in it. The money was in a gunny sack Reno Moore was guarding in his room. Bronc and Joe and me went out to the bar after the Brittons rode off. Joe wanted to chase them, but all I wanted was to ask him some questions away from the house. He might have had something to do with the Brittons getting out of jail. Maybe he knew the money was going to be on the stage. I haven't found out about that yet, but I'm saying that Joe was with me and Kline in the barn. Savvy?'

Matt nodded, and Glen went on. 'When we came back, Moore was knocked cold. The money was gone. The only other man in the house is Harlan Wells. You knew the money was here. I remember telling you. If it comes down to a choice between you and Harlan, I guess we all figure you're the one.'

'I tell you I didn't do it,' Matt whimpered. 'Search the room. You won't find it. I didn't

160

even know it was in a sack. I didn't know Moore had it. I wouldn't have known where to look.'

'That's right,' Kline said. 'He wouldn't have known.'

'He could have guessed,' Glen said. 'He knew Moore rides shotgun, and if he started looking around upstairs and saw Moore, he'd add it up. He's a drunk and a moocher and a liar, but he's not stupid.'

'Maybe we ought to look in his room,' Kline said uneasily.

'I said he wasn't stupid,' Glen said. 'He wouldn't have left it in his room. This is a big house. It could be anywhere.'

Tucker demanded, 'How much time are you going to waste?'

'How about it, Matt?' Glen asked. 'This is your last chance.'

'I can't tell you what I don't know,' Matt said hoarsely. 'For God's sake, Glen, don't turn this bastard loose on me.'

Glen stepped back and nodded at Tucker. He saw Kline turn away, he saw the sadistic pleasure in Tucker's face, and he knew he could not stand much of this, even as convinced as he was that Matt had the money.

Tucker's big hand struck Matt hard on the side of the face, the blow rocking his head, the sound as solid a *thwack* as if Tucker had struck the table. The other hand came down on the opposite side of Matt's face, rocking his head again and making the same sound.

'Just a beginning, old man,' Tucker said. 'I'm having a good time. The longer you hold out, the better time I'll have.'

Tucker closed his right fist and struck Matt in the mouth, bringing a spurt of blood. He cried out in pain, shrieking, 'I don't know. I don't know.'

The storeroom door was flung open and Susan ran into the kitchen, barefooted, her robe over her nightgown. 'Stop it, Joe,' she cried. 'Stop it.'

But Tucker acted as if he didn't hear. He raised his fist again. Susan grabbed his arm with both hands. Irritated, Tucker shook her free and struck Matt in the face again. Susan whirled to face Glen, screaming, 'Stop him, Glen. Stop him. You told me to stay in my room, but I couldn't with this going on. Can't you see what he's doing? He said he'd kill Pa if he came back. That's what he's trying to do.'

Glen caught Tucker's arm as he brought it back for another blow. 'That's all, Joe. If he had it, he'd have broken down before now.'

'I'll get it out of him,' Tucker shouted. 'Damn it, let me alone. I've just started.'

'You've started and you've stopped,' Glen said. 'I whipped you once tonight. You want me to do it a second time?'

Tucker's eyes locked with Glen's, and

again Glen saw the feral hatred that the man had for him. If Tucker ever got his hands on the money, their temporary alliance would be over and he'd kill Glen and run. At this moment Glen wasn't sure which was more important to Tucker, the money or Glen's life.

'You're soft, Logan.' Tucker jerked his arm free and turned away. 'Too soft for this job.'

Susan was on her knees in front of Matt, her head on his lap. She was crying wildly, almost hysterically, and Matt, blood running down his chin from a cut lip, was patting her on the top of the head.

'Let him go back to bed, Sue,' Glen said.

She lifted her head to stare at him, tears running down her face. 'You could have stopped him any time,' she cried. 'You let him do it. Isn't anything important to you except money?'

'Yes, Sue,' he said. 'The bank in Gold City is important. So are the lives and property and the businesses of the people in Gold City. The food in the mouths of the babies, too.'

She stared at him, not understanding. Turning, he walked into the dining room, knowing that it was no time to explain.

# CHAPTER NINETEEN

When Glen stepped into the dining room, he saw that Harlan Wells was standing at the foot of the stairs. He had his clothes on, but his hair was rumpled as if he had been asleep. When he looked at Glen, his eyes were so glassy and expressionless that Glen had the feeling Wells wasn't seeing him at all.

Kline was pacing restlessly around the dining room. When he saw Glen, he wheeled on him. 'What's the matter with us, boy? Have we all gone off our rockers? Is fifty thousand dollars enough to make us act like Apaches?'

'There are a lot of people in Gold City who are our friends and who'll be ruined if we don't find that fifty thousand dollars,' Glen said. 'I can stand losing what I've got in the bank, but it'll be hell on most folks.'

'I know, I know,' Kline said sharply, 'but my God, Glen, you just stood there and let that—that bastard beat old Matt to a pulp.'

'I was wrong,' Glen admitted, 'but I was sure Matt had it.' He looked at Wells, wondering, then asked, 'Harlan, did you hear or see anyone moving around upstairs tonight?'

'Yes.' Wells looked at Glen, his eyes not

quite as glassy as they were. He swallowed, trying to bring his thoughts together into a pattern of sanity, but they wouldn't quite track. 'I mean, I don't know, Glen. I just can't think straight. I must have had a real bad dream. It seems to me that I was planning to steal some of the money from the box to pay Buckner so I wouldn't lose the Home.'

Glen glanced quickly at Kline and brought his gaze back to the preacher's face. Something wasn't right with the old man. Glen had never seen him this way before. He had been under pressure for a long time, so much pressure that it was possible he had knocked Moore out and had taken the money and now could not remember. Such an act was so foreign to Wells's code of morals that he would not have done it if he had been perfectly normal, and it was obvious that Wells wasn't normal.

'The Britton brothers were here and they stole the box and killed Sam Kerwin,' Glen said, pointing to the body.

Apparently Wells saw the dead man for the first time. He turned his head, distressed. He said, 'I'm sorry. Sam was a good man.'

'The box was filled with rocks, Harlan,' Glen said. 'Reno Moore had the money upstairs in a gunny sack, but somebody knocked him out and stole it. Was it you?'

'No,' Wells said. 'I thought the money was

165

down here in the box. I remember planning to steal it and I knocked a chair to pieces so I'd have a leg to hit Moore with, then I knew I couldn't do it until the house was quiet, so I laid down and went to sleep. I woke up just now and then I wondered if I had done what I planned.'

Wells rubbed his forehead, trying to stir a memory that for the moment was lost in the dark recesses of his mind. He said slowly, 'No, I'm sure I didn't go into Moore's room, but I'd feel better if you'd come upstairs and search my room.

'All right,' Glen said, 'we'll do that. Just a minute.'

He stepped into the kitchen. Tucker stood with his back to the range, his bruised face still showing the savage anger that Glen had aroused in him when he'd made him stop beating Matt.

'Joe,' Glen said, 'move Kerwin's body into the hall and cover it with a sheet.'

Tucker said nothing. Glen wasn't even sure that he heard. He thought, *Maybe Kline's right. Maybe fifty thousand dollars is enough to put all of us off our rockers.*

'Joe, did you hear me?' Glen shouted.

'Yeah, I heard.'

'All right, then do it. And Joe, don't leave the house.'

'I ain't going nowhere till I get my hands on that dinero,' Tucker said sullenly, 'and when I do, I'm going fast and far.'

'Let me know when you start,' Glen said.

He crossed the dining room to the stairs and, climbing them, found Kline and Wells waiting for him in front of Moore's room.

'Reno's conscious,' Kline said.

'Have you talked to him?' Glen asked.

'No. He's got a hell of a headache. I hated to bother him.'

Glen stepped into the room. Moore stared at him, but he didn't move and he made no sound. Glen said, 'Reno, the money's gone. Somebody knocked you out and stole it. Did you see who it was?'

'No.' Moore put a hand to his head as if even speaking the one word hurt him, then he said slowly, 'Somebody knocked—I opened—the door—then the roof—fell in.'

'We're looking for it,' Glen said. 'If you think of anything, holler.'

Turning, he went back into the hall and followed Wells and Kline into Wells's room. The preacher stood at the foot of his bed, troubled eyes darting from one possible hiding place to another.

'I don't think I did it, Glen,' Wells said. 'I don't have any memory of doing it. You see, I never dreamed the money wasn't in the box downstairs. That's why I planned to go down there and hit Moore and take just enough of the money to pay Buckner.'

He picked up the chair leg and showed it

to Glen. 'I remember breaking up the chair so I'd have this for a weapon.'

'We'll look,' Glen said.

A search turned up nothing. Glen and Kline went through the preacher's suitcase. They examined the bureau. They tore the bed apart and found the broken fragments of the chair. That was all. There simply wasn't any money in the room.

Wells kept rubbing his forehead as if trying to draw something up into his conscious mind that eluded him. Finally he said, 'It seems to me there's something I ought to remember and can't, something that's important.' He paused, then asked, 'Was the money in gold or paper?'

'Paper,' Kline said.

'Then it could be on me,' he said, and started to undress. 'I guess this sounds ridiculous, Glen but I can't be sure I didn't do it. You see, I had planned it so carefully and I intended to take just part of it. Now I don't know how I could even have considered it, but I guess I thought that it was less of a sin to take a little than to take it all.'

He was rational now, Glen thought, but he was still worried about the hour or more which was a blank in his memory. He stood naked before them, a long-legged scarecrow of a man. As soon as Glen and Kline made a search of his clothes, they dropped the garments on the bed and he began to dress.

'You didn't do it, Harlan,' Glen said. 'Not unless you hid it in some other part of the house. That's what gets me. The money could be hidden in the house and we could hunt for a whole day and not find it. Even Susan or Molly couldn't think of all the places where it could be hidden, but I guess we've got to start looking.'

Glen turned, jerking his head for Kline to follow him. 'I want to get everybody up and I'll talk to them in the parlor,' Glen said when they were in the hall. 'It probably won't do any good, but I want everybody to know why it's important that the money be delivered to the bank in Gold City before it opens Monday morning. If we start talking, somebody might think of something that will help. Harlan may remember...'

'Hey, Mr. Logan.'

Glen whirled. Frosty Avery was standing in the doorway of his room, his nightgown reaching the floor. The sight of him touched off Glen's anger. He started towards the boy, saying, 'I told you to stay inside that room, didn't I?'

'I ain't out of it,' Frosty said.

Glen stopped. He heard Kline laugh softly, heard him say, 'I think he's got you there, Glen. He ain't disobeyed you.'

'If you're going to make me stay in this old room,' Frosty said, 'I can't show you something you'd like to see.'

Glen chewed on his lower lip, thinking for a moment that maybe the boy was strong enough to knock Moore out. He had done so many contrary things since he'd been here that Glen wouldn't put anything past him.

'Maybe you better let him out of his room,' Kline said. 'It's my guess he's got big ears. He might have heard something.'

'I sure did,' Frosty said. 'I know somebody stole the money. I heard somebody walking around up here while ago, but I didn't see who it was, then whoever it was left. After Ma was asleep, I sneaked out of the room.' He glared at Glen defiantly. 'If I hadn't, I wouldn't have found what maybe I'll show you.'

'All right,' Glen said. 'You don't have to stay in the room. Now what is it?'

Frosty cocked his head, staring at Glen as if not sure he could be trusted. He said, 'You told me you'd take a strap to me if I left the room again and I don't want to be whipped.'

'All right,' Glen said. 'I won't strap you. Just show us what it is.'

Frosty glanced past Glen at Kline and Kline nodded. 'He'll keep his word, son,' Kline said.

'Well, if you're sure you won't whip me.' Frosty stepped into the hall, still watching Glen for a hostile move. 'After it happened, I mean, after whoever it was went downstairs,

I got out of bed and looked into the old redhead's room. He was lying on the floor. I didn't see the sack of goober feathers anywhere, so I figured it had been stolen. Then I figured out maybe it had the money in it and that was why the old redhead got so mad because I wanted to look at the goober feathers.'

Frosty patted down the hall in his bare feet to a door across from Harlan Wells's room. 'I looked in all the rooms but I didn't find anything till I got here.'

He opened the door and pointed. 'Then I found that.'

The door opened into a small closet where Susan stored her spare pillows and blankets. There, on the floor, was a pile of Reno Moore's dirty shirts and the gunny sack. Glen dropped on his knees and tore the pile apart. The money wasn't there, not as much as a single greenback.

## CHAPTER TWENTY

The task of getting everybody out of bed, dressed, and into the parlor was not an easy one, with tempers as touchy as they were. Glen had built up the fire in the fireplace. It had been out for some time, and the air in the house was damp and cold. The wind, driving the rain hard against the house, seemed to find cracks around the doors and window casings, causing drafts which made the lamps on the oak center table flicker uneasily.

Glen stood with his back to the fireplace, taking his time rolling and lighting a cigarette. None of them, he thought, was very happy about being here. He wasn't sure he had a friend in the room. Even Susan who sat between Matt and Molly dabbed at her eyes with a wadded-up handkerchief and refused to look at him.

Well, he guessed he couldn't blame her. A few hours ago she'd been of a mind to marry him and throw Matt out for good, but when he'd permitted Joe Tucker to beat Matt as he had, he had turned her away from him and he made her an easy mark for her father again.

He threw his charred match into the fireplace and began to talk, telling them what had happened in Gold City and why it was imperative that the money be found and delivered to the bank before it opened Monday morning. He told them about the stratagem of filling the box with rocks and putting the money into the gunny sack and how it had fooled the Brittons and maybe Sam Kerwin, if he had actually tried to steal it when the outlaws shot him.

'Some of you know all of this,' he said.

'Some of you know only part of it. I thought we'd better begin by laying our cards face up on the table. Frosty, will you sit down?'

The boy had been restless from the moment he had come downstairs with his mother, walking around the room and sitting down and getting up and walking again until Glen couldn't put up with it any longer. Now Frosty dropped into a chair between Matt and the dining room door. He said, 'Mr. Logan, I want to help.'

'You've helped already,' Glen said. 'That's one thing I didn't tell everybody. Joe, Bronc, and me were in the barn when Reno was robbed. Frosty didn't see who it was because he was supposed to stay in his room, but he heard somebody walking around upstairs. After his mother went to sleep, he found the gunny sack and Reno's old shirt in a closet, but no money.'

'I'd like to help some more,' the boy said eagerly. 'Whoever took the money might have hidden it outside somewhere while you and Mr. Kline were upstairs. I want to go out and look for it.'

'Not till it's daylight which it's going to be pretty soon,' Glen said. 'Until it is, we'll look in the house. Now I've told you all of this so you'll know how important it is to get that money into Gold City. None of us are outlaws like the Brittons, but one of us, and maybe it was that way with Sam Kerwin,

173

couldn't stand the temptation of having that dinero under foot and not touching it. Let's say in a moment of weakness, one of you who is in this room slugged Reno and took it. Now if that somebody will get the money, I promise he won't be punished, but if he insists on trying to keep it, then he's a thief and he'll go to jail. We'll find the money if we have to tear the house down. It'll take some time, but we'll find it.'

No one stirred. Molly sniffed. 'You're acting like a fool, Glen. If I'd taken the money, I sure wouldn't trot out now and bring it to you.'

'I guess I didn't really expect anyone to,' Glen said, 'but I thought the guilty party should have a chance.'

He was wasting his time and he knew it. He looked around the room, still having no idea who the thief was. Reno Moore sat slumped in his high-backed rocker, a wet towel wrapped around his throbbing head. In spite of his respect for Moore, Glen could not overlook the possibility that the man had stolen the money, hit himself, and then pretended to be worse off than he was.

Molly sat with her big arms folded, scowling at Glen because she was still angry at being made to get out of bed in the middle of the night and dress. Matt stared at the floor, hoping that no one was paying any attention to him, and realizing, Glen thought, that he was still the most logical suspect in the room.

Now and then Susan looked at Matt anxiously and reached out and patted him on the arm. He would glance at her gratefully and then stare at the floor. Both Harlan Wells and Bronc Kline were watching and listening, and saying nothing. Joe Tucker, pacing back and forth along the windows, was almost as restless as Frosty.

Mrs. Avery was completely confused, so confused that she had been barely coherent when she first came downstairs. She'd said several times, 'Frosty and I didn't take the money, Mr Logan. We just wouldn't do a thing like that.' She wasn't much better off now.

Susan? Glen could not bring himself to accuse her, yet he knew that loving her was no cause for overlooking her. If there was any secret hiding place in the house that would not be found in a general search, Susan would know. But he did not suggest it; he had done enough to estrange her. Sitting there beside Matt, she seemed almost a stranger to Glen, something that a few hours ago he would have said was impossible.

'Well then,' Glen said, 'looks like we'll have to do it the long way. We've already gone through Harlan's clothes. I guess that's the place we'll have to start. We'll begin with Reno. He looks like he ought to be back in bed anyway. I want you women to go to Mrs. Avery's room and search each other.'

'Nobody's searching me,' Molly said. 'If you think I'm taking my clothes off in front of you or Susie or anybody else, Glen Logan, you're crazy. If I had a figure like Susie's got, I wouldn't mind showing it off, but with mine—'

She stopped, laughing uncertainly as if she wasn't sure whether what she'd said was a joke or not. Tucker said, 'She's got a lot to show off, Logan, and that's a fact. I don't blame her for not wanting to let anybody see it.'

Tucker had stopped pacing and now stood with his back to a window behind Bronc Kline. He leveled a finger at Matt. 'There's your man. You're a bigger fool than I figured you were, Logan. If you'd let me alone a little longer, I'd have beat it out of him.'

Glen shook his head, not wanting to discuss it. He told himself that Tucker would have been the most logical suspect if he hadn't been in the barn during the robbery. Perhaps, by some mysterious legerdemain, he had been in two places at once. It was about as logical as going back to Matt who, Glen was certain, would have broken the first time Tucker hit him if he had been guilty.

Mrs. Avery rose. 'I'm willing to be searched. I'd like to have my room and luggage searched, too, and then I'd like to go back to bed.'

Susan got up. 'I want you to search me, Mrs. Avery, if Mr Logan,' she paused, letting him feel the bite of her voice, 'will take our word for each other.'

He ignored her tone, nodding his agreement. He asked, 'What about Frosty, Mrs. Avery? You want me and Bronc to have a look at him?'

'Yes, then you men have got to examine my room and luggage. If you don't turn the money up somewhere else, you may decide you doubt Miss Girard's word and want to search me again.'

'No, we won't do that, Mrs Avery,' Glen said patiently.

She crossed to the archway that opened into the dining room, Susan behind her. Mrs Avery asked, 'Where did Frosty go? I thought he was sitting here.' She motioned to the empty chair beside Matt, questioning him with her eyes.

'He got up while ago ma'am,' Matt said. 'I didn't see where he went.'

'He must have gone upstairs,' Mrs. Avery said. 'I'll see. Miss Girard, will you look in the kitchen? Maybe he's getting himself something to eat.'

'Of course,' Susan said, and went into the kitchen.

'Molly,' Glen said, 'I hoped we'd get

everybody's cooperation, but we sure aren't getting yours. I can understand you're being modest, but you're stretching it. If I hadn't known you for a long time, I'd think...'

'Well, I'm glad to hear you say that,' Molly said belligerently, 'because you sure have known me a long time. You know I wouldn't steal a nickel. Joe and me have stayed here with Susie and worked for almost nothing just to help her out. What thanks do we get? You beat the puddin' out of Joe and now you're blaming me for stealing your old money. I didn't and I don't cotton to the notion of being blamed for it.'

'You're going to be searched just like Sue and Mrs. Avery,' Glen said, 'and we're going to look your room over. Now you've got the choice of cooperating, or Bronc and me will do the job if we have to hogtie you.'

Kline grinned as if he thought this would be quite an experience. Tucker stepped past the stage driver, his battered face turning dark with fury just as it had when Glen had made him stop beating Matt.

'You are a fool, Logan,' Tucker said. 'You talk about taking my wife's clothes off, but you don't do a damned thing about Matt. If you touch Molly, by God, I'll kill you. That's a promise.'

'Later,' Glen said wearily. 'Wait till I deliver the money to Gold City. Reno, you ready to...'

'Frosty isn't up here,' Mrs. Avery screamed, running down the stairs. 'Mr. Logan, you've got to find him.'

'No, I don't, Mrs. Avery,' Glen snapped. 'I've got more important things to do than look for a boy who's made nothing but trouble since...'

'Oh, Miss Girard, did you find him?' Mrs. Avery asked.

Susan had come into the dining room from the kitchen. 'No, I looked in all the back rooms and he's not there. I'll try the hall, but I expect he went outside.'

'In this rain,' Mrs. Avery wailed, 'and with those killers...'

'That's right, lady. Those killers have got him.'

Glen whirled toward the dining room. Jake Britton stood in the hall doorway, holding Susan in front of him against his wet slicker with his left arm, his right hand gripping his revolver, the muzzle pressed against her side. Glen's right hand swept downward for his gun and froze there, his fingers wrapped around the butt. Britton simply looked at him and shook his head.

'Better not, Logan,' the outlaw said, 'if you want this girl to live. You and Kline and anybody else who's toting an iron lay 'em on the table in front of you. Quick.'

Mrs. Avery's face was a ghastly green. She breathed, 'What about my boy?'

179

'The boy?' Britton said softly. 'Well Ma'am, I'll tell you. Bud's got him out in the barn. We'll swap him for the money. This time we ain't taking no rocks.'

## CHAPTER TWENTY-ONE

Matt Girard, from his chair near the archway leading into the dining room, watched what was happening as if he were a great distance from it, a spectator, the forgotten man. That was exactly what he was, he thought bitterly, and was reminded again of the clod lying in the road. A man could step on it or around it or over it. As far as Jack Britton was concerned, he seemed inclined to step over it. He glanced at Matt and after that ignored him completely as if he did not exist.

Matt watched Glen take off his gun belt and lay it on the table. Bronc Kline did the same. Reno Moore took a moment to get to his feet, and when he did, he swayed uncertainly, so pale that Matt thought he would faint, but he didn't. He walked to the table, put his gun belt beside the other two, and returned to his chair.

'All right.' Britton released Susan and gave her a push toward a vacant chair. 'I'll tell you just how it is. I ain't much on killing. Bud is, and he's the one who's got the kid. We didn't think the joke of filling the strongbox with rocks was very funny. If the money had been in it, we'd have been a long ways from here by now and you'd have been all right, but we took a look at what was in the box and we're back. Now you're not all right, not any of you.'

'But Frosty is just a boy,' Mrs. Avery cried. 'He didn't have anything to do with the box. Let him go.'

'Shut up,' Britton said. 'I'm talking, and right now I enjoy talking because I'm God-damned sore about having to ride back here to get what I thought we had in the box. This is our last job, then we're heading for Mexico as soon as we get the dinero. That's why we had to come back. We ain't likely to find fifty thousand dollars anywhere else just waiting to be picked up. Bud's got the kid and I've got the rest of you.'

Britton motioned towards Susan with his left hand. 'Take the girl there. Bud argued right along that we should have killed her before.' Britton glanced at Joe Tucker, his lips curling in distaste. 'We listened to you when we shouldn't have. Well, we sure don't need you now, and it ain't safe to leave anybody alive who runs off at the mouth like you do.'

'I don't any more,' Tucker said hastily. 'I ain't in much shape to talk.'

They'd both been in on the killing of Paul

Kelsey and Susan's mother, Matt remembered, and now apparently they had been together in this plan to rob the stage. Matt saw Glen's gaze linger on Tucker's face. *He knows*, Matt told himself. *He's finally got Tucker pegged.*

Tucker must have been the one who robbed Reno Moore, although how he managed to be in two places at once was more than Matt could figure out. He gingerly felt his battered, aching nose, then his swollen mouth. He should hate Glen he guessed, but he didn't. If Glen hadn't stopped Tucker, the man might have beaten Matt to death.

Matt heard Britton's derisive laugh, saw the contemptuous expression on the outlaw's face. He might just as well have said in words that Jake wouldn't be talking when he and Bud left with the money. Now his gaze swept the ground in front of him. He said, 'When I left Bud, I told him to give the kid half an hour. Some of it's gone. Five minutes. Ten minutes. I dunno. I don't care, neither. Now whoever knows where that dinero is had better go get it. Bud sure ain't gonna wait more'n the half hour I gave him.'

'We don't know where the money is,' Glen said. 'After you left, Tucker and Kline and me went out to the barn, thinking we'd go after you, and then we decided not to. While we were gone, somebody knocked Moore

182

out and stole the money. We haven't been able to find it.'

Britton laughed again. 'Now that's the damnedest hogwash I ever heard, but if you want to sit it out till you hear a gunshot from the barn and know the kid got it in the head, that's all right with me. If I have to do some more shooting to persuade you to find that dinero, I'll do it and I'll start with the girl.'

That hit Matt hard, probably harder than anyone else in the room because he believed what Jake Britton said and he doubted that anyone else did. If the Britton boys had done half the things they'd talked about in the Cerro jail, they were capable of murdering both the boy and Susan.

'You're talking like a fool,' Glen said, 'and I don't think you are a fool. You know that if you kill a boy and a girl like Susan, you'll have the whole country on your tail. You won't even get to the state line.'

'Don't worry about what will happen to us,' Britton said. 'Just get the dinero. I'm guessing that about half of the thirty minutes I gave Bud is gone.'

'You idiot,' Kline burst out. 'I'm the driver. I'm responsible for getting that money to Gold City, but I'd give it to you in a minute if it would save the boy's life.'

'Keep telling your lies,' Britton said. 'Only one thing counts. That's the money.'

'Let 'em plug the kid,' Molly said. 'Good

riddance, I'd say, after the hell he's raised around here.'

They all looked at her sharply, even Britton. Matt saw astonishment at her callousness on the faces of both Glen and Susan. Glen said, 'That's a hell of a thing to say, Molly.'

'Maybe it is,' she snapped, 'but if he'd stayed here like he was supposed to, he wouldn't be in this fix. Neither would we. I'm thinking about us. Britton wants the money, but we don't know where it is. Are you going to stand there, Glen, and let him wipe us out? That's what he'll do if we keep on like this.'

'What do you want me to do, rush him?' Glen demanded.

'It'd be better'n just sitting around waiting for him to massacree us. There's four of you men. He can't take all of you if you tackle him at the same time.'

'No, but I can sure get the girl,' Britton said. 'Shut your face, Fatty, or I'll start with you.'

Four of them, Molly had said. She hadn't counted Matt. Nobody ever counted him, he told himself. He knew then, and it came to him with a shock, that he was the only one who had a chance to get out of this room alive. He wouldn't be noticed because nobody ever noticed him.

Matt thought again of Glen asking him if

184

he had ever done a decent thing in his life. He remembered his feeble effort of sending money home to his wife when Susan was a baby. That was the best he could tell her, and it wasn't much to brag about.

Now Susan had enough of him. She'd picked Glen and she didn't give a damn about her own father. *He couldn't blame her.* That was the strange part of this whole thing. He was being honest with himself for the first time in years. He hadn't done a thing for Susan since he'd found her. Not a thing. But he could now. He could save her life, if he was lucky, and the boy's life. If he wasn't lucky, he'd lose his, but nobody cared about that. Nobody except Matt Girard.

There was this one strained moment, everybody staring at Britton, and Britton keeping his gun on Susan, a moment when all motion stopped and there was complete silence except for someone's gusty breathing. Then Mrs. Avery screamed, 'You animal! You sneaking, killing, thieving animal.' She jumped out of her chair as if she'd been shot forward by the release of a gigantic, coiled spring. She slashed at him with one hand, fingers curled like the claws of a cat, but she didn't quite reach his face. He hit her with the back of his left hand, the blow knocking her sprawling on the floor where she lay moaning.

'One more like that from any of you,'

Britton said angrily. 'Just one more move like that and I'll blow the girl's head off. Now I'm done fooling. Get that dinero and get it quick.'

Matt heard Britton's words from the dining room. He'd just got up and walked out. As Matt had thought, no one paid the slightest attention to him. He was in the kitchen when Glen said, 'I'll look for it. I'll start in the pantry. I'll go from there to the storeroom, then to Molly's room. It's in the house somewhere, but it'll take time to—'

That was all Matt heard. Glen was still talking when Matt slipped through the back door and crossed the porch. The rain hit him like a cold shower, drenching him that first minute. He ran across the yard towards the barn, heavy boots making a sloshing sound in the mud.

The door was open. He saw the dim light from the lantern. He reached the barn wall and stopped, leaning against it as he caught his breath, then he asked himself what he was doing here. What did he expect to accomplish against a killer like Bud Britton, with no weapon except his bare hands? If he wanted to live, he'd better get out here. Anywhere! Out into the rain and the darkness and keep going until he'd be far enough away so the Brittons wouldn't find him when daylight came.

From inside the barn he heard Bud

Britton's taunting voice, 'You got about five minutes, kid. You'd better start saying your prayers.'

'They don't know where the money is,' the boy shouted angrily. 'You're killing me for nothing. If they can't find it, they can't give it to your brother.'

Matt moved toward the door. He wasn't going anywhere. He didn't want to live. Not the way he had, a clod in the middle of the road. A drunk. A moocher. A small-time thief who was thrown into the jug because he stole a little whisky. He couldn't even be a big-time outlaw.

*One decent thing before you cash in your chips, Matt,* he told himself. *One decent thing that will make Susie think better of you when they bury you.*

The kid was just inside the door. Matt didn't know how far away the outlaw was, but if he rushed him, maybe the boy could run.

'Three minutes, kid,' Britton said.

The boy backed up a step, yelling, 'Do it now, you bastard.'

'Three minutes,' Britton said. 'That's what Jake told me to give you. That's what you're going to get.'

The boy wheeled to run. Britton laughed and lunged after him, knowing he could catch the boy. This was the cat-and-mouse game he loved, but just as he cleared the door, the gun in his right hand, Matt grabbed him around the waist and hauled him down into the mud.

Britton yelled in surprise, and perhaps fear, too. He fired a shot, the report deafening in Matt's ear. The outlaw kicked and squirmed and twisted, but Matt stayed on top, right hand jammed down hard on the outlaw's throat, his windpipe caught between Matt's thumb and forefinger.

Matt couldn't see the boy; he didn't know what he was doing or whether he was still running. He did know that his left shoulder stung, that he was wounded, but he didn't ease on his grip on Britton's throat. He shoved all the harder, thumb and forefinger closing against Britton's windpipe.

The outlaw threshed around, bucking and trying to throw Matt, but Matt was a-straddle of him, knees in the mud, and he stayed there. He knew he had to keep his advantage, that if he even let go, the outlaw would shoot him. He held Britton's right arm down with his left, his right not weakening for a second on Britton's throat.

The squirming and bucking became weaker. In the thin light from the lantern he saw that Britton's mouth was open, his tongue protruding from his lips, his eyes almost popping out of his head. Then Britton quit struggling and went slack, but Matt held his grip on the man's throat for another thirty seconds. When he did raise his hand, Britton was motionless.

Matt reached for the gun and took it from the slack fingers. He rose, the barrel lined on the outlaw's chest. He fired twice, both bullets slamming into the inert body. He backed up and leaned against the wall, breathing hard. He had killed a man and he was alive. He had saved the boy's life and maybe Susan's if he could get into the house in time. He had done a decent thing at last. He wanted to tell her—

Then his knees turned to rubber and he sat down in the mud. He felt the warm dribble of blood down his left arm where Britton had shot him. He closed his eyes. He was dying, he told himself, but Susan would know what he'd done. He'd bleed to death out here in the mud and the rain, but when they buried him, Susan would know. Maybe she would even cry a little when they shoveled the dirt into the grave on top of him.

## CHAPTER TWENTY-TWO

When Glen heard the first shot from the barn, he assumed that Bud Britton had killed Frosty, that Bud would be here in a minute or two. Apparently everyone in the room had the same thought. Mrs. Avery fainted and would have fallen out of her chair if Harlan Wells hadn't caught her and eased her to the floor.

'By God, Britton,' Kline said hoarsely, 'I hope both of you boil in hell. There's nothing lower than killing a boy, nothing.'

'Nothing except killing a woman,' Britton said. 'I guess none of you believed me when I told you we came back after the money. We ain't leaving till we get it. If it means rubbing out every one of you in this room, we'll sure do it.'

Glen was not far from the holstered guns on the table. Maybe two long steps, but it would take a moment to yank the pistol free from leather, a moment that would give Britton time to drop him and maybe another man. But what Molly had said a few minutes before was true. If all four of them, Glen, Joe Tucker, Bronc Kline, and Reno Moore rushed the outlaw, they could handle him.

Two more shots sounded from the barn. Britton laughed softly. He said, 'Bud never was one to rub out anybody quick and easy if he had plenty of time. I guess the kid's finished by now, so we'll wait till Bud comes in. I don't believe any of this hogwash you've been giving me about the money being gone, but I'll let you look, Logan. Bud can run herd on the rest of you. Just one thing. Bud ain't a patient man, so you'd better know

190

where to start.'

Britton's gun had been on Susan from the first. He kept it on her, but now for the first time he was plainly nervous. He was trying to watch both Susan and the archway into the dining room, apparently thinking Bud would come in and give him a hand.

Jake Britton didn't have the appearance of a church elder now. He was jumpy, the look of a killer on him, and Glen, who had been watching him carefully from the time he'd stepped into the room, recognized the danger of this growing nervousness. Any little move might set him off, but it would be worse when Bud came in. He wanted Susan dead. He would have killed her before if it hadn't been for his brother.

Glen eased forward a few inches, trying to catch Kline's or Tucker's eyes. He had no doubt now about Tucker's part in the whole plan, but Tucker knew as well as Glen did that the Brittons had no use for him; they would not go off and leave him alive. For the moment at least, Glen felt he could count on Tucker's help.

Kline and Tucker were both watching Britton, not Glen. Before he could get their attention, the front door banged open and a gust of air made the lamps flicker. 'About time,' Britton called. 'Bud, get in here and give me—'

Frosty ran across the dining room and

through the archway, yelling, 'That old man with the whiskers, the one that smelled so bad, he jumped Bud Britton and he choked him to death and now he's sitting out there in the rain.'

Frosty stopped, staring at Britton as if frozen. There was a strange moment that seemed to run on and on into eternity when all life in the room was suspended, as if everyone here was an actor in a tableau on a stage on which no one was supposed to move or say anything. If the situation had been less serious, Glen would have laughed at the ludicrous expression of incredulity that was on Jake Britton's face. He stood as if petrified, his mouth open, unable to believe what he saw before him.

Then the room exploded with both sound and movement. Molly threw herself in front of Susan. Jake Britton yelled, 'Bud ain't dead.' And Mrs. Avery, who had been flat on the floor, came out of her faint, and, seeing Frosty, screamed, 'Is that you, Frosty? Are you dead?'

Glen lunged towards the table. His fingers gripped the butt of his gun; his left hand held the holster while he jerked the Colt free, but it seemed to him he was inordinately slow, that Britton was swinging toward him and would shoot him before he had time to pull the trigger.

Frosty apparently sensed what was

happening before either Kline or Tucker did. He lunged toward Britton, yelling, 'Look out, Mr. Logan.' He was the closest to the outlaw, the only one in the room who could have reached him in time. He touched Britton's right arm with the tips of the fingers of his outflung hands, no more than a touch but enough to make Britton miss by inches.

Britton kicked the boy with a savage sideswipe of his right leg that sent Frosty spinning, but Glen had the brief interval of time that he needed. He fired just as Britton was bringing his gun into line again.

Glen's bullet caught the outlaw in the chest, a great hammer blow that knocked him back against the wall, his fingers releasing the gun. It hit the floor just as Kline reached him. The stage driver gripped Britton by both arms and held him upright a moment, then let him go, kicking his gun across the room.

'You drilled him right through the heart, Glen,' Kline said in awe. 'Hell, he was dead the second your bullet hit him. You're lucky or a damned good shot.'

'Lucky,' Glen said, feeling the sweat that broke through every pore in his body and ran down his face and chest and legs. He picked up his gun belt and strapped it around him, his fingers trembling so that it was a moment before he could finish buckling it. He shoved his gun into the holster and wiped his forehead with a sleeve. He tried to grin at Kline, but it was a sorry effort. 'Close, Bronc,' he said. 'Too close.'

Mrs. Avery hugged Frosty, crying over and over between sobs, 'Are you alive, Frosty? Are you sure you're alive?' Joe Tucker rushed across the room to Britton's body and kicked it, shouting, 'You double-crossing bastard, you'd have killed me.' Kline slapped Glen on the back and Reno Moore grabbed his hand and shook it.

Glen saw Susan was sitting bent forward in her chair, her head lowered. She was crying, her body shaking with each long sobbing breath. Glen started towards her, knowing how she must feel now that this terrifying half hour was over, but before he reached her, Matt Girard made a dramatic entrance, shouting, 'Bud Britton shot me. I'm dying. I'm bleeding to death.'

Matt was dripping wet, he was smeared with mud, and his face was gray and pinched with fear. He tottered through the hall door into the dining room and on into the parlor. There he collapsed, falling forward so hard that he jiggled the pictures on the wall. Susan ran to him and, kneeling by his head, felt it and then picked up a wrist to check his pulse. Glen knelt on the other side. With his pocket knife he slashed the sleeve away from the wound. He raised his head and looked at Susan. He said, 'He's a faker. Look at that.

Just a scratch. He may be scared to death, but he's sure not bleeding to death.'

Frosty escaped from his mother's arms and tugged at Glen's sleeve. He said, 'Mr. Logan, he's no faker. I started to run out of the barn. That Bud Britton was telling me I only had three minutes to live if his brother didn't get the money. I didn't know the old man was outside, but he grabbed Britton just as he came through the door and fell on top of him and choked him to death. Then he got Britton's gun and shot him twice. That outlaw would have killed me sure if it hadn't been for him.'

Matt's eyes flicked open. 'You're sure it ain't bad, Glen?'

'I'm sure. Sue will wash it out and put a bandage on it and you'll be all right.' Matt sat up and Glen held out his hand. 'I never thought I'd live to see the day when I'd call you a hero, but I'm seeing it.' Pleased, Matt shook hands with him, and Glen added, 'The fact is a few minutes ago I never thought I'd live to see another day.'

Frosty was shaking Glen's arm again. 'Something else you ought to know, Mr. Logan. Bud Britton did a lot of bragging out there in the barn. He said that fellow there, that Tucker, was the one who fetched the gun to 'em so they could get out of Cerro jail. Another fellow in Gold City named Ed Thorn had told Tucker that this money was coming on the stage. Thorn and Tucker was to get a third of it, but the Brittons wasn't figuring to give 'em any.'

Glen had guessed it was that way. He rose, reaching for his gun as he said, 'We'll take you to the sheriff in Cerro, Joe. You didn't get the money, but you'll sure get a jolt for helping the Brittons break jail.'

Tucker grinned mockingly. 'I don't figure I will, Logan. Turn around.'

'Get your hand away from your gun butt, Glen,' Molly said.

She stood in the dining room beside the table, a double-barreled shotgun in her hand. She was wearing a slicker and had one of her husband's hats on her head.

'It ain't the Brittons you need to worry about now,' Molly went on. 'It's the Tuckers, and I sure like it better this way. I've got the gun and I've got the money.' She patted the two bulges under her slicker. 'Now Joe and me are leaving. Susie, go put your riding duds on. We're taking you along.'

'Now I know what I was trying to remember after I woke up,' Harlan Wells said. 'It was Molly opening the door and looking into my room.'

'You're a little late, preacher,' Molly said. 'I seen through that trick about the goober feathers, but I didn't know which room Moore was in, so I had to look. I hit him and took the money out of the sack and threw it and the shirts into the closet. The money was in our room all the time. You'd have found it easy if you'd looked. I never got a chance to hide it.'

'You're out of your mind, Molly,' Glen said, remembering Kline's remark about the fifty thousand dollars being enough to send any of them off their rockers. Right now Molly didn't look like the hard-working, good-natured Molly Tucker who had been Susan's right arm all this time. 'You know Susan won't go with you and you ought to know you won't get very far.'

'Who's coming after us?' she demanded. 'Dead men ain't riding horses. Joe, go saddle up. Susie thinks she's not going, but she is.'

'I don't know, Molly,' Tucker said. 'She's sweet on Logan. If we knock him off...'

'Go on, damn it,' Molly screamed. 'I can handle Susie. She's like our own daughter, ain't she? What have we hung around here for all these years?'

'To make a haul,' Tucker said. 'Now we've got it, so let's ride.'

'Susan's going with us, I tell you,' Molly said fiercely. 'I never liked her ma and I hated Paul Kelsey, but I wouldn't have killed 'em for a third of the five thousand dollars Kelsey had buried in the yard like you done. This was what I was waiting for, something big that was worth killing for. No more

197

cooking and washing dishes and getting up afore daylight, Susie. We'll live like human beings for a change. We'll have somebody waiting on us. Damn it, Joe, go saddle those horses.'

'Glen's right,' Susan said. 'I won't go with you and Joe. Oh, Molly, what's happened to you. I thought Joe might do something like this, but not you.'

'Oh no, not me,' Molly said derisively. 'I'm patient. That's all. I knew we'd get a crack at something good, but I didn't figure on the Brittons horning in. I was a mite worried for a while, but my good friend Glen took care of him.'

'And Matt,' Glen said, knowing that if there was any chance for them at all, it would come from making her talk, or breaking her away from her husband, and that seemed unlikely. 'Matt got rid of Bud. Remember?'

'Matt!' she spat at him. 'That tub of guts! Joe, we're doing this wrong. Get the rope that's in our room and we'll tie 'em up, then we'll burn the house. That's better'n shooting 'em. Susie, you've got to go with us. I can't do it to you. Joe'n me love you. We've stayed here to help you. Don't you see?'

'Love me?' Susan stared at Molly as if she were a stranger. 'You're going to murder my father and the man I want to marry and you talk about loving me. Why, you've gone

198

crazy, Molly.'

That was exactly what had happened, Glen thought as Tucker left the dining room to get the rope. From the look on Tucker's face, Glen suspected that he didn't know what had happened to his wife. He was wearing a gun. Glen wasn't sure whether it was Kline's or Moore's, but he had taken one of the revolvers from the table.

Once they were tied in a chair, there would be no chance for any of them. As crazy as Molly was, her one weak spot was still Susan. Now, staring at the woman's moonlit face that had been turned bright red by the excitement and at her feverish eyes, Glen could not think of any way to take advantage of that weakness.

Joe Tucker was as evil as the Britton boys had been, but he was sane. Molly wasn't, and that, Glen knew, was what made this moment more dangerous than any time Jake Britton had held his gun on them.

## CHAPTER TWENTY-THREE

A weird sense of unreality gripped Glen. He wondered if he was having a nightmare with this recurring scene of danger and violent death which waited just ahead for all of them. No, this was no nightmare. He had only to look at Molly's face, at those glittering, feverish eyes, to know how terrifyingly real this was.

A combination of miracles had saved them before, of Matt Girard somehow finding courage to tackle Bud Britton and of Frosty getting away and running into the house and distracting Jake Britton's attention and Glen getting his gun out of the holster in time to shoot the outlaw, again with Frosty's help. But what kind of miracle could save them from a crazy woman with a shotgun who was obsessed with the idea of burning the house and everyone in it except Susan?

The rain had stopped and dawn was moving into a reluctant sky. The river would go down within a matter of hours so it would soon be possible for a man on a horse to ford the stream with the money and take it to Gold City in time to save the bank. Funny he would think of that now, with the twin eyes of Molly's shotgun fixed on one person and then moving to another.

A great weight of absolute despair settled down upon Glen. He had considered rushing Jake Britton, and he would have if he could have given the nod to Kline and Tucker, but going against a revolver in the outlaw's hand and charging a double-barreled shotgun were two different things. Molly would blow a man's head off with one load and have the second left for anybody who was fool enough to try again.

Tucker came in with the rope. Molly said, 'Put it down, Joe, and go get the can of coal oil out of the storeroom. We'll move 'em over against that wall yonder,' she nodded at the east wall of the parlor, 'and we'll tie 'em into their chairs. Then we'll empty the coal oil on the floor. We'll give 'em a fire they'll never forget.'

Tucker looked at his wife, plainly not knowing what to make of her, then turned and walked back into the kitchen. It would probably be only a matter of hours before Tucker killed her and took the money. He'd know he would have to travel fast and Molly was not a good rider. She would be a drawback for him he could not afford.

More than that, Molly was crazy; she was giving orders as if she was drunk with power, but Joe Tucker was not a man who let any woman dominate him. They would take Susan, and what would happen to her? Molly considered her a daughter, but Glen was not at all sure that was Joe Tucker's feeling toward her.

'Molly,' Susan cried, 'you just can't do a terrible thing like this.'

She stared towards Molly and stopped when Molly said, 'Don't come no closer, honey. I don't want to hurt you but I might have to if you keep coming.' The shotgun moved to cover Glen. 'Or maybe I'll hurt your sweetheart. I don't like him much. I don't like nobody you do. I guess I'm kinda jealous.'

Glen stared at the twin bores of the shotgun aimed directly at him, black, malignant eyes that would tear his body apart if she pulled the trigger. Molly would enjoy killing him, he thought. What she had just said about being jealous explained a good many things such as her hatred for Matt Girard and not interfering with the murder of Susan's mother and Paul Kelsey.

'Hurry up with that oilcan,' Molly yelled. 'It's getting daylight. We ought to be moving.'

'I can't find it,' Tucker yelled back.

'It's in the storeroom,' Molly bellowed. 'In the corner behind the churn.'

Glen looked at the others. Everyone in the semicircle that faced Molly seemed to be frozen except Susan who stood poised like a bird about to take off in flight. She was the one person in the room, Glen thought, who had a chance to save them, but she didn't know what to do, with Molly's shotgun covering Glen. He couldn't have told her what to do if he'd had a chance to tell her anything.

Glen's pulse was hammering in his head; a strange, heavy object lay deep down in his belly that felt as if he'd swallowed a cold stone. A chill struck him and he shivered,

202

and at the same time sweat ran down his forehead, but he didn't dare wipe it away.

His gun butt was only inches from his right hand, but with Molly's mad, glittering eyes fastened on him, he knew it would be suicide to make a move of any kind. Even if someone else, Bronc Kline or Reno Moore, had made a try for his gun, it would have meant Glen's death first and the man who went for his gun second. So, knowing that, neither of them tried.

'I found it,' Tucker called from the storeroom.

''Bout time,' Molly growled. 'All right, back up against the wall, all of you but Susan. Not too close together.'

Glen took one step toward the wall. Suddenly Frosty who had been standing motionless beside his mother, danced toward Molly, calling, 'Mamma, she sure is a fat woman, ain't she? Those old biscuits of hers made my stomach ache.'

Molly swore. 'I've had all of that brat I'm going to take,' she snapped.

She stepped toward Frosty, her gaze switching from Glen to the boy. Raising a big foot, she kicked him in the stomach and knocked him flat on his back. Mrs. Avery screamed and leaped at her.

Molly tried to whip the barrel of the shotgun around to cover Mrs. Avery, but Susan, who had inched closer to Molly when

Frosty started dancing and yelling, rushed at the big woman and knocked the barrel toward the floor.

One blast went off, splintering the boards at Molly's feet, then both Susan and Mrs. Avery were wrestling Molly for possession of the shotgun. Harlan Wells and Reno Moore charged in then, a step behind the two women. The four of them brought Molly to the floor, Moore finally getting the shotgun away from her, but she still kicked and plunged and threw out her great arms in punishing blows.

Glen and Kline thought of Tucker at the same time. They drew their guns and raced towards the kitchen door. Joe Tucker was part way across the kitchen when he heard the shotgun go off. He dropped the oilcan and drew his pistol. When he saw Glen and Kline running along the side of the dining room table toward him, he fired once, but he hurried it, perhaps panicking, and his bullet went over Glen's head.

Glen cut Tucker down with two shots, the second driving through the bridge of his nose and slanting upward through his brain, killing him instantly. Kline, behind Glen, didn't get a chance to fire.

Glen holstered his gun and for a moment stood looking down at Joe Tucker who for a time had played second fiddle to his wife. That was a strange thing, for it was not like him at all. He could not have claimed temporary insanity; he would have burned them alive just as Molly was going to do.

Glen turned away, feeling no remorse or regret for having shot the man. Killing him was an execution; it was long overdue, and if it had not come so late, Susan's mother and Paul Kelsey would be alive today.

Overcoming Molly was much the same as wrestling a berserk cow, but they subdued her by sheer weight and numbers. Glen helped hoist her great bulk into a chair and then tied her feet together, her hands behind her back, and then lashed the rope around her middle and the back of the chair. Mrs. Avery fainted for a second time and Susan fled into Glen's arms. He held her for a long moment, letting her cry until the hysteria passed.

There were things to do after that. The bodies were moved to the hall and laid out beside Sam Kerwin's. Kline carried Mrs. Avery upstairs and placed her on the bed, telling Frosty to stay right beside her so she could see he was all right when she came to.

'If she don't have a nervous breakdown, I'll be surprised,' Kline said when he came downstairs. 'She's sure been through it tonight.'

Matt, finally convinced that his wound was not serious, walked to Susan's room and immediately lay down. Glen had built a fire, and as soon as the water was hot, Susan washed and bound the bullet slash Bud Britton had given him.

The money was taken from Molly who cursed them until she was out of breath, then she sat glowering at them in silence, hating them with every fiber of her massive body. They spread the money on the dining room table and counted it, then sacked it when they found it was all there.

They sat back and looked at each other, Glen and Kline and Moore and Harlan Wells, the early morning sunlight pouring through the east windows. They were glad just to be alive, but they were tired, too, and not fully used to the idea that the danger and violence that had threatened them for so long was behind them.

'Man and boy,' Kline said, 'I've been handling money for thirty years or more. I worked for an express company when I was a kid. I rode shotgun for a while, and I've been driving now for quite a spell, but this is the first time I've ever seen so much money in one pile.'

'It's like a big dose of poison,' Moore said. 'Four men dead. Molly crazy as a bedbug. Me with a cracked skull. All of us scared to death. This has been a night.'

Harlan Wells motioned toward Molly. 'We've all known her for quite a while,' he said. 'I guess you knew her the best, Glen. I think Joe has always been a bad one, but I don't believe Molly was until that money was brought into the house last night. Then when she had a chance to think about how much was there and what it would buy, I believe she went out of her mind. I know because I had a taste of that same kind of insanity.'

'It's what made Ed Thorn do what he did and end up shooting himself,' Glen said. 'It's what makes Bill Buckner do some of the things he does. Now I've got an idea about him. How do you feel, Reno?'

'I can ride, if that's what you mean.'

'It is,' Glen said. 'The river will come down within a few hours now that the rain's stopped. We can ford it with horses below where the bridge was.' He turned to Wells. 'Bronc will have to stay here for a couple of days until he can ford the river with the coach, but today he might just as well go to Cerro. The bodies have to be taken to town, the sheriff has to be told what happened, and Molly has to go to jail. It's a two-man job. Will you help, Harlan?'

'I'd be glad to,' the preacher said, 'but if I don't get to Gold City, I can't raise the money...'

'You can't raise it in the time you have anyway,' Glen said. 'But maybe I can. That's why I want to go with Reno instead of having you or Bronc go. I've got money in

Buckner's bank and I've got some important friends in town that Buckner will have to listen to. I propose to go to him with Reno and tell him the money was stolen and will he give a reward to get it back. Will five thousand dollars be enough?'

Wells grinned. 'Just right.'

Glen looked at Moore. 'It's blackmail of a sort, Reno. Think we can pull it off?'

'Sure we can,' Moore answered. 'Before we get done, we'll make that old goat look so small we can pull him through the knothole in Gold City.'

'Good,' Glen said. 'I'll go see if I can help Sue turn out some breakfast.'

'Glen,' Moore said as Glen rose from his chair at the table. 'This kid Frosty. He's a gutty little devil, but I don't savvy him. He was so damned ornery, then he saves our hides tonight.'

'About three times,' Harlan Wells said. 'Twice, anyway.'

'Did he know what he was doing?' Moore asked. 'I mean, that he was risking his life or was he just showing off some more?'

'Let's say he had been with his mother too much,' Glen said, 'and then let's say he learned something by being with men and about being a man himself. Maybe it would be fit and proper, Reno, for you to go upstairs and shake hands with him. Kind of bury the hatchet.'

'I'll do it,' Moore said. 'I sure will.'

Susan was sitting beside the bed talking to Matt when Glen stepped into the room. She rose when she saw who it was. She smiled at him as he went to her and put an arm around her. He asked, 'Matt, what did you figure you'd accomplish walking out into the rain and jumping Britton the way you did? Were you just being brave?'

'Brave?' Matt said. 'No, I ain't brave, Glen. I never will be and I never was. Maybe I wasn't thinking much at all, but I knew I was the only one who could walk out of that room and not be noticed. I done it, and then I wanted to do a decent thing before I died. I couldn't forget that question you asked me. I figured that if I done something out there, you might get a chance to jump Jake. That's just what you done.'

'That's right,' Glen said.

'Did I finally do a decent thing?' Matt asked eagerly.

Glen smiled as he looked down at this dirty, lying, foul-smelling man who had almost succeeded in completely wasting his life. He probably would never change, but last night he had earned the right to sit on the porch the rest of his life if that was what he wanted to do.

'You sure did, Matt,' Glen said. 'You sure did.'

'Look, Glen,' Susan said, nodding at the

209

window. 'Maybe that's a sign, like the rainbow is supposed to be a promise from the Lord.'

The clouds had rolled away from the craggy peak of Storm Mountain and the early morning sunlight was sharp and bright upon it. Glen said, 'I guess it is. That makes it a good time to decide something. You want to sell this place and help me run my hotel?'

'No. I love it here, Glen. I want to stay.'

'All right, then I'll sell out and move in with you.'

'Oh Glen, that's what I've wanted for so long.'

She reached up and pulled his head down and kissed him. Glen winked at Matt who grinned back. Glen said, 'It's quite a girl you've got here, Matt.'

'Yeah,' Matt said. 'She's quite a girl.'

**Wayne D. Overholser** has won three Golden Spur awards from the Western Writers of America and has a long list of fine Western titles to his credit. He was born in Pomeroy, Washington, and attended the University of Montana, University of Oregon, and the University of Southern California before becoming a public school teacher and principal in various Oregon communities. He began writing for Western pulp magazines in 1936 and within a couple of years was a regular contributor to Street and Smith's WESTERN STORY and Fiction House's LARIAT STORY MAGAZINE. BUCKAROO'S CODE (1948) was his first Western novel and still one of his best. In the 1950s and 1960s, having retired from academic work to concentrate on writing, he would publish as many as four books a year under his own name or a pseudonym, most prominently as Joseph Wayne. THE BITTER NIGHT, THE LONE DEPUTY, and THE VIOLENT LAND are among the finest of his early Overholser titles. He was asked by William MacLeod Raine, that dean among Western writers, to complete his last novel after Raine's death. Some of Overholser's most rewarding novels were actually collaborations with other Western writers,

COLORADO GOLD with Chad Merriman and SHOWDOWN AT STONY CREEK with Lewis B. Patten. Overholser's Western novels, no matter under what name they have been published, are based on a solid knowledge of the history and customs of the American frontier West, particularly when set in his two favorite Western states, Oregon and Colorado. When it comes to his characters, he writes with skill, an uncommon sensitivity, and a consistently vivid and accurate vision of a way of life unique in human history.